Ralph Waldo Emerson

The Early Poems of Ralph Waldo Emerson

Ralph Waldo Emerson

The Early Poems of Ralph Waldo Emerson

ISBN/EAN: 9783337407834

Printed in Europe, USA, Canada, Australia, Japan

Cover: Foto ©Andreas Hilbeck / pixelio.de

More available books at **www.hansebooks.com**

THE
EARLY POEMS

OF

Ralph Waldo Emerson

WITH AN INTRODUCTION BY

Nathan Haskell Dole

T. Y. CROWELL & COMPANY

NEW YORK

CONTENTS.

CONTENTS.

LIFE OF RALPH WALDO EMERSON.

IN the early years of the nineteenth century, when Boston was as yet only a comfortable little seaport town, and its principal streets still gave room for gardens and cow pastures, there stood at the corner of what is now Summer and Chauncy streets a gambrel-roofed wooden building, shaded by elms and Lombardy poplars, and surrounded by ample grounds. This was the parish house of the oldest church in Boston, called the First or "Old Brick Church."

The minister of this church and occupant of this mansion was the Rev. William Emerson, who on the 25th of May, 1803, wrote in his diary: "This day, whilst I was at dinner at Governor Strong's, my son Ralph Waldo was born."

The Rev. William Emerson was one of the notable men of his day. Although his life was cut off at the early age of forty-two, he had accomplished a work the influence of which is still definitely, if unconsciously, felt, and always will be felt in the culture of Boston. Science and learning as represented by the Lowell Institute, literature as represented by the Athenæum, art as represented by the Museum, point back to that vivacious, liberal-minded, and eloquent

young minister. He had been settled in the town of
Harvard at a yearly salary of less than six hundred
dollars, but Boston heard him preach, wanted him and,
in 1799, bought him off from the Harvard parish for a
bonus of a thousand dollars, giving rise to the epigram
perpetrated at the expense of the Old Brick Church :
"You bought your minister and sold your bell."

William Emerson traced his descent from Thomas
Emerson, who emigrated from England to America in
1635, was thrifty, and left a large estate for those days.
His son John, minister at Gloucester, was the common
ancestor of Phillips Brooks and Wendell Phillips.
His son Joseph, preacher successively at Wells, at
Milton, and at Mendon, married Elizabeth, grand-
daughter of Peter Bulkeley, a wealthy and learned
dissenting minister, who founded Concord and Concord church.   Edward, son of Joseph and Elizabeth,
married Rebecca Waldo, and his son Joseph married
Mary Moody and had ten children, the ninth of whom
was William, who was the minister at Concord, and
built the Old Manse celebrated by Hawthorne. When
he died at the early age of thirty-three, his widow
married his successor, the Rev. Ezra Ripley, who was
a kindly and wise step-father to the lively young
William, his mother's only son. It is said that he
had no drawing to the ministry, but, on hearing Dr.
Ripley pray for the fulfilment of his mother's desire,
he studied divinity and was settled at Harvard at the
age of twenty-three. His letters are full of wit and
vivacity. He was extremely fond of society and liked
to sing and to play on the bass viol. He was too poor

to keep a horse, but in 1796, when his salary was only $330.30, he married Miss Ruth Haskins, sold his bass fiddle, took boarders, taught, and worked his farm. At the time of his death he was receiving $2500 a year, thirty cords of wood, and the rent of his house. He raised potatoes, corn, and other vegetables in his garden on Summer Street. He was the founder of the Philosophical Society, and the leading member of the Anthology Club, which established a library, a museum, a course of lectures, and a monthly magazine.

Ralph Waldo Emerson was eight at the time of his father's death. The parish voted to continue the salary to the widow for six months longer, to pay her $500 a year for seven years, and permitted her to occupy the parish house for more than three years. She took boarders, did her own work, and managed to educate the children, as she felt that they were born to be educated. The distance between her little vessel and the lee shore of poverty was very small. Mrs. Ripley found the family one day without any food, except the stories of heroic endurance with which their aunt, Mary Moody Emerson, was regaling them. Ralph and his brother Edward had but one overcoat between them, and had to take turns going to school.

This aunt, Miss Emerson, was a thorn in the spirit for the whole family. Of great intellect, of lofty views, ambitious, religious, sceptical, a burning brand in the household, she stimulated, she exasperated, she made herself and every one about her unhappy. She wanted every one but herself to be orthodox. Emerson said of her: "She tramples on the common humanities all day, and they rise as ghosts and torment her all night." Mr. Charles Eliot Cabot says: "She was an ever-present embodiment of the Puritan conscience." Her influence on the Emerson children was, on the whole, injurious. Even Ralph Waldo, who was less susceptible to it than the others, felt it severely.

Ralph was sent to school before he was three years old. At ten he writes his Aunt Mary of his studies in the Latin School, which were supplemented by two hours' attendance at a private school where he learned to write and cipher. Once or twice he played truant during this midday recess of extra work, and was punished for it by imprisonment with bread and water. He was not a brilliant scholar, nor was he inclined to mingle with his associates in play. He never owned a sled, and, though there was a good pond for skating not far away, he did not learn to skate till he was a freshman in college. According to Dr. Furness he held aloof from "Coram" and "Hy-spy," and other sports, simply because from his earliest years he dwelt in a higher sphere. He could not remember the time when Emerson was not literary in his pursuits. When he was thirteen his uncle, Samuel Ripley, asked him how it was that all the boys disliked him and quarrelled with him.

In 1814 the price of provisions became so high in Boston that Mrs. Emerson and her family took refuge in Concord with Dr. Ripley, with whom they spent a year. On their return to Boston they lived in a house on Beacon Hill lent by its owner in exchange for board for his wife and children. Emerson remembered driving the cow to pasture on Carver Street. That year he was reading " Télémaque " in French and Priestley's lectures on history, and his letters are pretty well peppered with original verse. In October, 1817, he went to Cambridge, having passed a very good examination, and his mother rejoiced because he did not have to be admonished to study. He was appointed President's Freshman, a position which gave him a room free of charge. He waited at Commons, and this reduced the cost of board to one quarter, and he received a scholarship. He added to his slender means by tutoring and by teaching during the winter vacations at his Uncle Ripley's school in Waltham. Mr. Conway says that during his college course his mother moved to Cambridge and took student boarders, but Emerson had his room in the college buildings, occupying 5, 15, and 9, Hollis, during the last three years, respectively.

Even in his fourteenth year he was described as being "just what he was afterward, kindly, affable, but self-contained, receiving praise or sympathy without taking much notice of it."

He was fonder of desultory reading than of regular study, and naturally came into some disfavor with the authorities. In mathematics he confessed himself "a hopeless dunce," and laughingly declared that a possible English congener, William Emerson of Durham, a famous mathematician, must have appropriated all his talents in that line. "I can't multiply seven by twelve with security," he added.

George Ticknor, who taught modern languages, and Edward Everett, Greek professor, gave lectures, and Emerson attended them with profit. He took two Bowdoin prizes for dissertations, and the Boylston prize of $30 for declamation. He graduated just above the middle of a class of fifty-nine, and had one of the twenty-nine commencement parts, but, disgusted at its insignificance, took no pains to learn it, and had to be frequently prompted. He was not entitled to admission to the Φ. B. K. Society, but he was elected class poet, and his poem was regarded as a superior production. His future seemed indefinite. All he would promise was "to try to be a minister and have a house." The house was for his mother, so that he might "in some feeble degree repay her for the cares and woes and inconveniences she had so often been subject to on her son's account alone."

After he graduated he for two years assisted his brother William in a school for young ladies established in his mother's house, and when William went to Göttingen to study divinity, he remained another year in sole charge. During these three years he earned nearly $3000 and was enabled to help his mother and brothers. But he always remembered his terrors at entering the school, his timidities at French, "the infirmities of his cheek," and his occasional admiration of some of his pupils, and his vexation of spirit when the will of the pupils was a little too strong for the will of the teacher.

He regretted that his teaching was perfunctory. He wished that he had shown his pupils the poems and works of imagination which he himself delighted in. Then teaching might have been for him also "a liberal and delicious art." He always wondered why the poorest country college never offered him a professorship of rhetoric. He wrote in his journal: "I think I could have taught an orator, though I am none."

In 1823 Mrs. Emerson hired a house on Canterbury Lane, also called Light Lane, Dark Lane, or Featherbed Lane, Roxbury, about four miles from the State House. In Franklin Park a tablet in the Overlook on Schoolmaster Hill commemorates the fact that Emerson there, stretched out beneath the pines, wrote his poem, "Good-by, proud world; I'm going home." His letters from there show that the teaching in town, which he still kept up, was not much more irksome than the communion with nature which had been recommended to him. "I cannot find myself quite as perfectly at home on the rock and in the wood as my ancient, and I might say infant, aspirations led me to expect," he wrote on the 19th of June of that year. "When I took my book to the woods I found nature not half poetical, not half visionary, enough. . . . I found that I had only transplanted into the new place my entire personal identity, and was grievously disappointed."

In 1825 Emerson wrote his aunt that Channing was "preaching sublime sermons every Sunday morning in Federal Street." The influence of Channing may have determined him to fit for the ministry, though his brother William, much to his mother's grief, had found it impossible to subscribe to creeds and had decided against that profession. But Ralph Waldo confessed that, while he inherited from his "sire a formality of manners and speech," he also "derived from him or his patriotic parent a passionate love for the strains of eloquence." He therefore elected to study divinity. His brother William advised his going to Göttingen, but he wrote: "Unless I take the wings of the morning for a packet, and feed on wishes instead of dollars, and be clothed with imagination for raiment, I must not expect to go." And like a true philosopher — like the fox philosopher of the story — he adds: "It might not do me any good."

Certain lands in the city had increased in value and a little money was forthcoming from them; so he decided to go to Cambridge, where "the learned and reverend" had consented to admit him to the middle class. In February, 1825, on the eve of leaving his Canterbury home, he wrote that he had "learned a few more names and dates, additional facility of expression; the gauge of his own ignorance, its sounding-places and bottomless depths." He added that his "cardinal vice of intellectual dissipation — sinful strolling from book to book, from care to idleness" — was his cardinal vice still — was a malady which "belonged to the chapter of incurables."

He took a floor room in the cold, damp northeast corner of Divinity Hall, and within a month was obliged by ill health and weak eyes to suspend his studies. He went first to Newton and worked on his

Uncle Ladd's farm. Here he fell in with an "ignorant and rude laborer" who was a Methodist, and it is chronicled that Emerson's first sermon was founded on this man's dictum, that "men were always praying and all their prayers were answered." But he added as a saving clause, "We must beware, then, what we ask!"

In the summer he instructed a few private pupils, and in September took charge of a public school in Chelmsford, which he left at the beginning of the next year to relieve his brother Edward of the care of his school in Roxbury, and then in April he returned to Cambridge, where his mother had again taken a house. He opened a school there and had among his pupils Richard Henry Dana, 2d, but he was afflicted with rheumatism and threatened with lung complaint.

He managed to attend some of the lectures at the Divinity School, and made a show of keeping along with his class. But he afterward declared that if the authorities had examined him on his studies they would not have passed him. They did not examine him, and he was "approbated to preach" by the Middlesex Association of Ministers in October, 1826, and on the fifteenth of that month delivered his first public sermon at Waltham.

As cold weather came on, he was obliged to go South. The deferring of his hopes made him heartsick. Mr. M. D. Conway says he preached in Charleston, which had the only Unitarian pulpit south of the Potomac. But the weather was cold and he took a sloop to St. Augustine, where he spent the winter "parading the beach and thinking of his brother barnacles at a distance." He was amused at the theological and civil manners of the place, where "the worthy father of the Catholic Church was arrested and imprisoned for debt, where the president of the Bible Society was notorious for his profanity, and its treasurer, the marshal of the district, combined meetings of the society with slave-auctions." Emerson made the acquaintance of Prince Achille Murat, "a philosopher, a scholar, a man of the world, very sceptical but very candid, and an ardent lover of truth." He long remembered him as "a type of heroic manners and sweet-tempered ability."

When he reached Alexandria after a direfully tempestuous voyage, he wrote his aunt that he was not a jot better or worse than when he left home. In this same letter he describes how when he reads Walter Scott, a thousand imperfect suggestions arise in his mind, which, if he could give heed, would make him a novelist; and, when he chances to light on a verse of genuine poetry, even in the corner of a newspaper, a forcible sympathy awakened a legion of little goblins in the recesses of his soul. and if he had leisure to attend to the fine tiny rabble, he would straightway be a poet. He confessed that in his day-dreams he hungered and thirsted to be a painter.

On his return he "supplied" for some weeks at the First Church, during the absence of its regular minister. Then in the autumn of 1827 he supplied for Mr. Hall at Northampton, where he made the acquaintance of the Lymans. Mrs. Lyman was a descendant of

Anne Hutchinson, whom Emerson's ancestor, Peter Bulkeley, had helped to drive out of Massachusetts; but a warm friendship quickly sprang up between the brilliant and beautiful woman and the pale young student, whom she called an angel unawares.

He had several "calls" to accept permanent positions, but his health was still so uncertain that he refused them all, and lived at Cambridge a desultory life, "lounging on a system," writing a sermon a month, strolling, courting the society of laughing persons, and trying to win "firmer health and solid powers."

He had not as yet shown evidence of remarkable ability; his brothers Edward and Charles entirely eclipsed him. He never jested (so Dr. Hedge said), was slow in speech and in movement, and was never known to run. Yet when his brother Edward, "the admired, learned, eloquent," lost first his reason and then his health, and died in self-imposed exile, Emerson wrote in his journal that he had little fear for such an evil, even in the line of the constitutional calamity of his family; "I have so much mixture of *silliness* in my intellectual frame, that I think Providence has tempered me against this."

He had preached temporarily at Concord, N. H., and there he met Miss Ellen Louisa Tucker, the daughter of a former Boston merchant. She had greatly impressed him, but he thought he had "got over his blushes and his wishes." But when he met her again in December, 1828, he "surrendered at discretion." "She is seventeen years old and very beautiful by universal consent," he wrote his brother William.

In March of the following year he was settled as colleague of the Rev. Henry Ware, Jr., over the Second or Old North Church, and in September was married and established in a house in Chardon Place. His happiness and success seemed to him too great to last. His intuitions were not ill founded. He found himself unable to administer the Communion in its concrete oral form, and when the church refused to let him continue the service, dropping " the use of the elements," he resigned, and his resignation was accepted by a vote of thirty against twenty-four. It must have been a relief to him to be free, for all that savored of ritual was distasteful to him, and even extempore prayer was irksome. He did not excel in the usual pastoral relations. It is related of him that when he was summoned to administer consolation at the bedside of a Revolutionary veteran, and showed some awkwardness in the matter, the dying man rose in his wrath and exclaimed, " Young man, if you don't know your business, you had better go home." Even the sexton of the church declared that in his opinion he was not born to be a minister.

But his ability in the pulpit was marked, and many of his congregation greatly regretted the step that was forced on him. He had recently suffered the loss of his young wife, who even before her marriage was threatened with consumption. She died in February, 1831. He was like a ship adrift. But great schemes were floating in his mind. One of them was the establishment of "a magazine of his ownty-donty," in which there should be no coöperation, but only his personal individuality to unify it.

Again his health broke down. He was disheartened, and felt that the doom of his race was on him. At first it was suggested that he should go to the West Indies and visit his brother Edward, but at the last moment he found that a 236-ton brig was about to sail for the Mediterranean : he took passage on her and was landed at Malta on the 2d of February, 1832.

In his diary written on the vessel one can read the influence of Carlyle. Speaking of the clouds, he says : " What they said goest thou forth so far to seek — painted canvas, carved marble, renowned towns ? . . . Yes, welcome, young man, the universe is hospitable ; the great God who is love hath made you aware of the forms and breeding of His wide house. We greet you well to the place of history, as you please to style it, to the mighty Lilliput or ant-hill of your genealogy." And so on quite in the style of " Sartor."

From Malta, where he with a tame curiosity looked about La Valetta, he crossed to Sicily, spent several days in sight of Etna, drank of the waters of Arethusa, plucked the papyrus on the banks of the Anopus, visited the Catacombs, heard Mass in the ancient Temple of Minerva, and fed on fragrant Hyblæan honey and Ortygian quails ; but he felt tormented by his ignorance, wanted his Vergil and his Ovid, his history and his Plutarch. " It is the playground of the gods and goddesses." " The poor hermit who with saucer eyes had strayed from his study " found himself

somewhat at a loss in those "out courts of the Old
World." "Some faces under new caps and jackets,"
he says, "another turn of the old kaleidoscope."

He was not sure in the noise and myriads of people, amid the grandeur and poverty that he saw, that
he was growing much wiser or any better for his travels. "An hour in Boston and an hour in Naples
have about equal value to the same person."

Even his judgment of people remind one of Carlyle
in his peevish days. He hoped he should not always
be "yoked with green, dull, pitiful persons." The
"various little people" with whom he had been
"cabined up by sea and land" may have been all
better and wiser than he ; still they did not help him.
He longed for a teacher. He would "give all Rome
for one man such as were fit to walk" there.

At Florence he dined and breakfasted with Landor,
who, he thought, did "not quite show the same cali-
ber in conversation as in his books." He hoped for
better things of Carlyle, to whom he was pilgriming
through all such inanimate trifles as coliseums and
duomos. Even Venice he called "a great oddity, a
city for beavers . . . a most disagreeable residence ";
and Paris was "a loud modern New York of a place."
"Pray, what brought you here, grave sir?" "the mov-
ing Boulevard" seemed to ask him. A lecture at the
Sorbonne, he complains, was far less useful to him
than a lecture which he should write himself !

He stayed about three weeks in London. He attended service at St. Paul's. "Poor church," is his
only comment. He visited Coleridge and Bowring

and John Stuart Mill, and still in quest for Carlyle reached Edinburgh, where he .preached in the
Unitarian chapel, and at last, after peculiar difficul-
ties, discovered his ideal living quietly at Craigenputtoch — the youth he sought he called " good and wise
and pleasant," and his wife, " a most accomplished,
agreeable woman." " Truth and peace and faith dwell
with them." His visit with them he called " a white
day in his years." Carlyle, on his part, always declared it was the most beautiful thing in his experience at Craigenputtoch. Yet even Carlyle was not
the long-sought master. In the deepest matters the
Scotchman had nothing to teach the Yankee. He
had met with men, he wrote, of far less power who
had got greater insight into religious truth.

But the interview on both sides was pleasing and
resulted in a lifelong friendship.

At Rydal Mount he paid his respects to Wordsworth,
and was not offended by the old poet's egotisms.[1]
Having reached Liverpool, he confided to his journal
his gratitude to the great God who had led him in
safety and pleasure through " this European scene —
this last schoolroom " in which He had pleased to
instruct him. The sight of Landor, Coleridge, Carlyle, and Wordsworth, though he realized that not
one of them was " a mind of the very first class," had
comforted and confirmed him in his convictions. He
felt that he would be able to judge more justly, less
timidly, of wise men for evermore.

[1] For Emerson's own account of his experiences see " English Traits."

It is odd and sounds almost prehistoric to read Emerson quoting the prediction that "the time will come when the ocean will be navigated by merchantmen by steam."

With health restored and established, he reached New York early in October, after a voyage which lasted more than a month; and, having rejoined his mother at Newton, where she was then living, he began to preach and lecture as occasion offered. On the second Sunday after his return he occupied his old pulpit in the Second Church and for four years supplied at various places. He might have had a call to New Bedford, but as he stipulated that he must not be expected to administer the Communion or to offer prayer unless the Spirit moved, the church withdrew its invitation. His first lecture was delivered in November, 1883, before the Boston Society of Natural History. His early lectures were on scientific subjects and before scientific bodies.

He was expecting to have his wife's share of her father's estate, and this expectation was soon satisfied, so that he made sure of a yearly income of about $1200, and he was meditating more seriously than ever the adventure of a periodical paper which should "speak the truth without fear or favor." This materialized afterward in *The Dial*.

In the summer of 1834 he was the chosen poet for the Φ. B. K. Society, and the verses contained a word portrait of Daniel Webster. His brother Edward, who had just died, had been Webster's private secretary and tutor to his children. He went to Bangor to preach for a few Sundays, and wrote to Dr. F. H. Hedge that he was seriously thinking of trying to persuade a small number of persons to join him in a colony thirty miles up the river; but this visionary project of a forest hermitage was never carried out, and in October he went to live in Concord, which was his home throughout the rest of his life. He lived with his mother in the Manse until, in 1835, having become engaged to Miss Lidia Jackson of Plymouth, he bought at a bargain the Coolidge house, which he said was a mean place, and would be till trees and flowers should give it a character of its own. It was a square mansion set rather low in a field, through which flowed a brook down to the sluggish Concord River.

In September he was called on as a townsman to deliver a discourse on the two hundredth anniversary of the incorporation of the town, and he made special investigations for the purpose of imparting historic value to it. Two days after this event he drove to Plymouth and was married there at the Winslow house, which belonged to his bride. She would have liked to live in Plymouth, but he preferred Concord, and had written to her that " he was born a poet, though his singing was very husky and for the most part in prose," and therefore must guard and study his rambling propensities. Concord, he intimated, gave him sunsets, forests, snowstorms, and river views, which were more to him than friends, but Plymouth ! —" Plymouth is streets !"

In the winters of 1835–1836, besides supplying the East Lexington church, he began a course of ten lectures on English literature, and this made such a favorable impression that henceforth his career was assured. Not only was the subject-matter original and unique, but the judgments expressed were sound, and the delivery was marked by a peculiar charm which those who heard him never forgot:

> *" You are filled with d·light at his clear demonstration,*
> *Each figure, word, gesture, just fits the occasion!"*

said Lowell.

In 1836 Emerson helped to introduce to American readers Carlyle's " Sartor Resartus," which had the distinction of selling the first edition and a thousand copies besides, before it was put into book form in England.   His efforts in this practical direction elicited the little sneer in Lowell's " Fable for Critics," where he speaks of Emerson in these words : —

> *His is, we may say,*
> *A Greek head on right Yankee shoulders, whose range*
> *Has Olympus for one pole, for t'other the Exchange.*

Or again a little farther down he says he is composed of " one part pure earth, ninety-nine parts pure lecturer."

Lowell was even more severe on Emerson's poetry. After comparing his rich words to "gold nails in temples to hang trophies on," he says, his —

> *Prose is grand verse, while his verse, the Lord knows,*
> *Is some of it pr —   No, 't is not even prose.*

And he goes on : —

> *In the worst of his poems are mines of rich matter,*
> *But thrown in a heap with a crash and a clatter.*

When Lowell was editor of the *Atlantic Monthly*, Emerson sent him his mystic "Song of Nature." But Lowell returned it to him, stating that certain lines in it would offend the religious susceptibilities of the community. The lines particularized were those where Homer, Shakespeare, and Plato were united with Christ in one : —

> *Twice have I moulded an image,*
> *And thrice outstretched my hand ;*
> *Made one of day, and one of night,*
> *And one of the salt sea-sand.*
> *One in a Judæan manger*
> *And one by Avon stream,*
> *One over against the mouths of Nile,*
> *And one in the Academe.*

Emerson was amazed, and took the poem to Miss Elizabeth Hoar, who was always his kindly censor, and asked her if she could see anything offensive in the lines.

Emerson said : " She read them carefully, but failed to help me out, concluding that they were not to be altered and must be allowed to stand. So they will not trouble the readers of the *Atlantic*."

In 1836, on the day of the two-hundredth anniversary of the founding of Harvard College, Emerson and others met and discussed the state of philosophy and theology. A few days later a project ripened of founding a periodical to embody their views. Thus was started *The Dial*, which became the organ of the so-called transcendental movement, though the first number did not appear till July, 1840. Emerson's book, " Nature," is regarded as " the first document of that remarkable outburst of Romanticism on Puritan ground." It was published in September, 1836. Only a few copies were sold, and twelve years elapsed before a new edition was called for. But it was violently attacked by the champions of orthodoxy. Yet Dr. O. W. Holmes said Emerson took down men's "idols from their pedestals so tenderly that it seemed like an act of worship."

This year was saddened by the death of Charles Emerson, whom Ralph Waldo called " his brother, his friend, his ornament, his joy, and pride"; he "has fallen by the wayside or rather has risen out of this dust," he wrote in his journal; " now commences a new and gloomy epoch of my life. . . . Who can ever supply his place to me ? "

Charles Emerson was a born orator, who would have conferred on the Republic rare gifts of genius had he lived. Emerson's lament for him was one of the most touching things he ever wrote. This same year Emerson's first child, a boy " of wonderful promise," was born, but he lived only five years.

Within a few years Margaret Fuller and Amos Bronson Alcott came to him in Concord ; but Margaret Fuller, in spite of her genius and in spite of his admiration for her genius, always " froze him to silence," and he had the same effect on her when they were on the point of coming nearer. But for Alcott he had the highest praise. He called him the most extraordinary man and the highest genius of his time. This admiration lasted till the end of his life. In his later

days, when aphasia had so shattered his mind, there
is a pathetic picture of him talking over the fence
with Alcott with much of his old-time fluency; but
in the afternoon Alcott returned and brought back to
Emerson the philosophic bread that had been cast on
the waters so abundantly.   And Emerson, oblivious to
the fact that it was his own, dilated with admiration,
and exclaimed: "What a wonderful mind my friend
over yonder"— he could not remember his name—
"has!"

Thoreau was also one of Emerson's intimates, and
frequently shared his week-day walks.   Yet, curiously
enough, Emerson objected to printing Thoreau's
"Winter Walk" in *The Dial*.   Hawthorne lived for
four years in Concord, occupying the old Manse, but,
though he was a great walker, he is known to have
walked with Emerson only once, when they went together to visit the Shakers at Lebanon.   Emerson
said of Hawthorne, "Alcott and he together would
make a man!"

Emerson's reading, as might be imagined, was pe-
culiarly eclectic and erratic.   Mr. Cabot says he cared
nothing for Shelley, Aristophanes, Don Quixote, Miss
Austen, Dickens, Dante, or French literature.   He
rarely read a novel.   But the Neo-Platonists and the
Sacred Books of the East particularly engaged him,
and were the inspiration of many of his mystic lines.

Mr. Cabot says he lived among his books and was
never comfortable away from them, yet they did not
enter much into his life.

In 1836, having finished a course of twelve lectures

on the "Philosophy of History," he was asked to repeat them in various places, though the one on "Religion" gave some offence. The substance of these twelve lectures afterward was included in his first series of "Essays." He still officiated occasionally as a minister, but the reception of his Phi Beta Kappa oration on "The American Scholar," given August 31, 1837, cut the last thread of attachment. Lowell said of this: "It was an event without any former parallel in our literary annals. . . . What crowded and breathless aisles, what windows clustering with eager heads, what enthusiasm of approval, what grim silence of foregone dissent." Dr. Holmes called that oration "Our Intellectual Declaration of Independence."

In February he relinquished his charge at East Lexington, though his wife mourned "to see the froward man cutting the last threads that bound him to that prized gown and band, the symbols black and white of old and distant Judah."

A still greater shock came from the discourse which Emerson delivered in July, 1838, on the graduation day of the Divinity School. The *Advertiser* led in a bitter attack on him. Emerson described the stir that it made as "a storm in our wash-bowl." But it nearly resulted in excluding him from the lyceum as well as from the church ; and he felt a little disturbed that it had placed him on an undeserved pedestal as a champion of heresy.

But his annual courses of lectures in Boston were not less popular. Theodore Parker wrote of the first one, given in the early winter of 1839: It "was splendid — better meditated and more coherent than any theory I have ever heard from him. Your eyes were not dazzled by a stream of golden atoms of thought such as he sometimes shoots forth — though there was no lack of these sparklers."

Emerson had at first declined to have editorial control of *The Dial*, but when, after two years of uphill struggle, Margaret Fuller relinquished it, he took hold most unwillingly and kept it along for two years more at some expense of money and much expense of worry. It lived till April, 1844. His own known contributions numbered not far from fifty. There may have been half as many again.

During three years the question of negro emancipation was coming to the fore. Emerson was at first more interested in having the right of free discussion upheld than in the deeper question beyond. In November, 1837, he spoke on Slavery in the vestry of the Second Church in Concord, but the Abolitionists thought his tone was too cool and philosophical; but in 1844 he delivered an address in the Concord court-house in celebration of the anniversary of the liberation of the British West India Island slaves. All of the Concord churches refused to open their doors to the convention, so Thoreau secured the court-house, and is said to have rung the bell himself. And this time Emerson's trumpet gave forth no uncertain sound. He took a wise and common-sense view about woman suffrage, and, though he was not inveigled into any of the labor associations, such as Brook Farm and

Fruitlands, in which his enthusiastic friends tried to interest him, he was not averse to developing a simpler and fairer way of living, and he invited the Alcotts to come and make common cause with them for a year. But Mrs. Alcott was wiser than the rest, and prevented the experiment being tried.

These years were not free from pecuniary anxieties. The most he ever received for a course of ten lectures before 1847 was $570. The country lyceums paid $10 and expenses. His family was increasing, and the town levied heavy taxes on him. His tax-bill for 1839 was more than $160. So he was constantly in debt, and his chief resource was the lecture field, though it revolted his nature to sell "good wine of Castaly." In 1843 he spent the whole winter away from home, lecturing in New York, Baltimore, and other places. Moreover, in order to preserve a hold on nature, he bought fourteen acres of woodland on Lake Walden, and this was a pecuniary burden for several years.

It comes with a sense of relief, like a sea-breeze on a sultry day, to read of him taking a vacation from that strenuous life of the platform by going to the seashore. He wrote his wife: "I read Plato, I swim, and be it known unto you, I did verily catch with hook and line yesterday morning two haddocks, a cod, a flounder, and a pollock, and a perch. . . . The sea is great!" This touch of the sea, "inexact and boundless," may be detected in the oration which he tried to write at Nantasket for delivery at Waterville, Me. But "the heat and happiness" of his inspiration were extinguished, as he long afterward confessed, by the cold reception with which it met. It was either at Waterville or in a Vermont town, perhaps both, that the minister at the end of the discourse prayed to be "delivered from ever again hearing such transcendental nonsense from the sacred desk." Afterward he went a number of times to the Adirondacks, where some of his sweetest poems were composed. He bought a rifle, but never used it.

Mr. Cabot says that lecturing, after all, was not the mode of utterance to which he aspired. Verse was, because he could get a larger and freer speech in rhyme. Some of his poems had been circulated, a few had been printed. And in December, 1843, a bookseller proposed to him to furnish a volume of his verses. But four years passed before the crucial impulse came to remedy "the corrigible and reparable places in them," and to put them together. "It was a small venture," he said. "My poems did not pay. My cranberry meadows paid much better." And when he made this remark he added, "My poems fell dead in England."

In 1847 he made his second journey to England, visited Carlyle for four days, and was amazed at "the great and constant stream" of his talk. "Carlyle and his wife," he says in a home letter, "live on beautiful terms." He breakfasted with Rogers, drank tea with James Martineau, and found profuse kindness and hospitality in Preston, Leicester, Chesterfield (where he dined with Stephenson, "the old engineer who built the first locomotive"), Birmingham — every-

where he went.   At Edinburgh, where he lectured
several times, he met all the notables, — " Christopher
North," David Scott the painter, who made a portrait
of him, Mrs. Jeffrey, Lord Jeffrey, Thomas De Quincey,
and many more.

Still more brilliant was the society he met in London, — Macaulay, Bunsen, Milman, Milnes, Hallam,
Lord Morpeth, "Barry Cornwall," Lord and Lady
Ashburton, Thackeray, Disraeli, Lord Palmerston,
and Tennyson.   He was elected a member of the
Athenæum Club, where he found some of the best
men of England.

In May, 1848, he crossed to Paris and saw something of the Revolution and went to the theatre, where
he heard Rachel.   He complained humorously that
his French was far from being as good as Madame de
Staël's.

He returned to London in June and gave a course
of lectures, at which he had most aristocratic audi-
ences and dined with great lords and brilliant authors.
But the pecuniary returns were smaller than he had
reason to expect.   For the Marylebone course of six
he got only £80 instead of £200.

On his return to America he made the larger part
of his income by lecturing.   But he looked on the
whole business as rather unseemly.   He thought that
it was a pity to drive young America to lecture, and
as to the lecturer, he said that the "dragging of a de-
corous old gentleman out of home was tantamount to
a bet of $50 a day that he would not leave his library
and wade, and freeze, and ride, and run, and suffer

all manner of indignities, and stand up for an hour each night reading in a hall."

But he did it, and his pictures of travel in the West in the pre-Pullman days are like the stories of the martyrs. Here we find him sleeping on the floor of a canal-boat, where the cushion allowed him for a bed was crossed at the knees by another tier of sleepers as long-limbed as he, "so that in the air was a wreath of legs"; again occupying a cabin, though in company with governors and legislators, and a cold of minus fifteen degrees. Again, flying through the forests of Michigan in company with college professors and wolverines. And again, ferried across the Mississippi in a skiff, where "much of the rowing was on the surface of fixed ice, in fault of running water."

In 1849 Emerson's separate addresses and "Nature" were published in one volume, and the next year came "Representative Men."

That year, 1850, also brought with it the Fugitive Slave Law, and Emerson's voice was lifted nobly against it. He here made a magnificent attack on Daniel Webster, for whose genius he had such an admiration as "the best and proudest, the first man of the North." He believed in confining slavery to the slave states, and then gradually and effectually making an end of it. He called on "the thirty nations" to do something besides ditching and draining. Said he, "Let them confront this mountain of poison and shovel it once for all down into the bottomless pit. A thousand millions were cheap!"

History proved the truth of his prophetic words.

At Cambridge he repeated the words containing these wise counsels, but was so interrupted by hisses and cat-calls that he could not go on. The college authorities, like the clergy and merchants, were generally Southern in sentiment.

When John Brown was in prison under sentence of death Emerson had the courage to call him "that new saint, than whom none purer or more brave was ever led by love of men into conflict and death — the new saint awaiting his martyrdom." His attitude on that burning question of the day militated against his success as a lecturer. Invitations to speak were withdrawn, and in 1861 at the meeting of the Massachusetts Anti-Slavery Society " the mob roared " whenever he tried to speak, and he had to withdraw. That was in his native Boston! The war also brought poverty pretty close to Emerson as to so many others. His books did not sell, his income from lecturing almost ceased, his real estate was unproductive, and he found himself struggling with the problem, how to pay three or four hundred dollars' worth of debts with fifty.

On January 1, 1863, when Lincoln's Emancipation Proclamation went into effect, a Jubilee Concert was given at the Music Hall, and Emerson read his "Boston Hymn." The time which he gave himself for its composition was so short that he was in despair, lest he should not be able to do anything worthy of the occasion. But the inspiration flowed and a new treasure was added to English literature.

That same evening a gathering of the faithful took place at the house of Major George L. Stearns, at

Medford, who perhaps did more than any man in Massachusetts to help along the cause of emancipation, who spent money like water, and himself raised the first two regiments of colored troops. Mrs. Stearns, who, with intellect as keen as ever, still lives to speak eloquently of those great days, thus tells the story of that epic gathering.

"Mr. Emerson was persuaded to repeat his poem, the 'Boston Hymn,' the original manuscript of which the Rev. Samuel Longfellow promptly begged of the author.

"It was a brilliant assembly, filled with exultation over the decree of emancipation which had been wired from Washington. The certainty of this great measure Wendell Phillips had announced as he entered the drawing-room. Instinctively the company burst into the John Brown song, greeting the newly unveiled bust of the martyr of freedom, which the sculptor J. Q. A. Brackett had just made.

"It was past midnight when the guests departed, every heart glowing with the sublime event, rejoicing with a mighty joy that deliverance from slavery at last had come."

Then occurred one of those charming little episodes so characteristic of Emerson's thoughtfulness and simplicity. Mrs. Stearns thus relates it : —

"Mr. Emerson and his friend, Mr. Alcott, remained overnight.

"When the hostess asked Mr. Emerson his preference of sleeping rooms, he said, 'Let Mr. Alcott and myself have the same room, then Vesta will have only *one* instead of *two* beds to make in the morning.'"

Another characteristic anecdote of the same kind may be related here, also from Mrs. Stearns's recollections : —

" On one occasion, after we had been visiting the Emersons, when we were preparing to drive home, the evening being rather chilly, for it was autumn, Mr. Emerson brought his overcoat from the hall, and, holding it up by the collar, said, ' I am always a little suspicious of the warmth of ladies' garments, the evening is cool, and the drive is one of seventeen miles ; it will oblige me, Mrs. Stearns, if you will put on this overcoat, and wear it home. It can be recommended for warmth if not for elegance.'

" It was beautiful hospitality and consideration, but I instinctively drew back, saying : —

" ' Oh, Mr. Emerson, how can I dare to wear the Lion's Skin !'"

He could only be persuaded to withdraw the overcoat by being assured that sufficient wraps were stowed away in the carriage. "I have regretted," says Mrs. Stearns, "the modest scruples that hindered the wearing of the Poet's Coat, just for once."

In 1863 he was appointed one of the visitors to West Point, where John Burroughs, seeing him, took him to be "an inquisitive farmer." In 1866 he was granted the degree of Doctor of Laws by Harvard and elected one of the overseers. The following year he was orator for the Φ. B. K. Society — "not now," says Mr. Cabot, "as a promising young beginner from whom a fair poetical speech might be expected, but as the foremost man of letters of New England."

It was at this time rumored that he was drifting back from heretical to more conventional opinions in religious matters; and it is stated on good authority that, when it was proposed to dispense with compulsory prayers at Harvard, Emerson's vote prevented the innovation from prevailing. But he authorized his son to announce that he had not retracted any of his views.

Three years later he was gratified to be invited to give a course of university lectures in Cambridge, and for this he prepared his sketches of " The Natural History of the Intellect," but he was not satisfied with his attempt to make a system of philosophy. The fruit of Emerson's intellect was not cohesive, but granular, and his thoughts are not easily moulded into a consecutive logical form. Hence it was possible for him to begin a lecture or end it anywhere. In his latter days I remember hearing him read a paper before the Radical Club. Every little while he would stop, saying he had gone far enough. But the audience and his daughter would persuade him to continue. But when he finally paused, the subject had been neither begun nor exhausted. His mind was like a carbon point; when the electricity was turned on, it gave out light, and it was always ready to shine.

He repeated his Cambridge course the next year, but felt that he had not succeeded as he had hoped to do. In a letter to Carlyle he called it "a doleful ordeal," and when it was concluded, accepted with alacrity an invitation to visit California on a six weeks' trip with near friends and in the most delightful circumstances.

After 1870 the decay of his mental powers, particularly of his memory, was very noticeable. He spoke of himself as "a man who had lost his wits." His last effort of composition was an introduction to Plutarch's "Morals" edited by Professor Goodwin. He compared it carefully with the original Greek, which he was able to read.

In July, 1872, he had just returned from Amherst, where he had delivered an address, when he discovered that his house was on fire. The neighbors rushed to his aid and succeeded in saving the books, manuscript, and furniture; but the house was ruined by fire and water, and Emerson himself contracted a feverish attack from exposure to the dampness.

Friends rushed to his aid in even more substantial ways. Mr. Francis Cabot Lowell brought him an envelope containing $5000. Nearly $12,000 more were contributed to rebuild the house, and while the work was in progress he was persuaded to make another journey abroad, to visit London, Italy, and Egypt. He saw Carlyle once more and dined with the Khedive. He and his daughter went up the Nile to Philæ, but on the whole he was disappointed with the sacred land: "the people despise us," he wrote, "because we are helpless babies who cannot speak or understand a word they say; the sphynxes scorn dunces; the obelisks, the temple-walls, defy us with their histories which we cannot spell."

The journey did him good, however, and on his return to Italy he began to work on a new edition of his poems. In Paris he saw Renan, Taine, Turgenief, and James Russell Lowell; in England he declined all invitations but one to speak, but he breakfasted with Gladstone, and saw Browning and many other notables.

When he reached home in May he was surprised and touched by the spontaneous welcome of his townspeople. The church bells rang, the whole town assembled — babies and all — and he was escorted with music to his new house, where a triumphal arch had been erected. He found his study unchanged, but many improvements had been introduced in the restoration of the house.

The following year his anthology of collected poems, "Parnassus," was published, and he was asked to be one of the candidates for the lord rectorship of Glasgow University. For this he received five hundred votes. Disraeli was elected, however.

In March, 1875, he went to lecture in Philadelphia, and had a delightful visit with his old friends, Dr. Furness and Samuel Bradford. The next month he made a little speech at the unveiling of Mr. Daniel C. French's "Minute Man," and this is believed to be the last piece written out with his own hand. After this time Mr. James Eliot Cabot served as his literary guide, shaping his lectures, and combining them, and helping him to arrange for the complete edition of his works.

Still occasionally reading from his lectures, still en-

joying the serene calm of old age, where even his infirm-
ity of memory may have made it all the serener, free
from all worriment, he lived on till the spring of 1882,
when he died of pneumonia on the 27th of April, at
the very end of his seventy-eighth year.

One could fill many pages with testimonials of the
influence of Emerson with contemporary descriptions
of the man and his beneficent life.

Henry Crabbe Robinson declared that he had one
of the most interesting countenances that he had ever
beheld — a quite disarming combination of intelligence
and sweetness.   N. P. Willis grew enthusiastic over
the voice, which he said was the utterance of his soul
only, and his soul had sprung to the adult stature of
a child of the universe.

Dr. Holmes said : " He was always courteous and
bland to a remarkable degree ; his smile was the well-
remembered line of Terence written out in living
features."   No one who ever heard him speak will
forget the play of his features, the lighting up of his
eyes with a rapt inner illumination, the emphatic
stamp of his foot when some weighty thought re-
quired enforcement.   He was one of the great souls
of the century, and his works will be for all time a
source of inspiration to young and old.   They are
indeed a mine of thought, all the more valuable, perhaps, that they are not welded into a system.

Many enthusiasts consider him to have been the
greatest poet America has yet produced.   Technically
this thesis can never be supported.   His disdain of
mere form led him to produce verses which read with

heaviness and halting, but the beauty of the thought atones for missing symmetry and freshness of rhyme, and Emerson as a poet will always have an audience of admirers and some worshippers, oblivious of his verse's fault. Once when some one praised his poetry Emerson interrupted, "You forget; we are damned for poetry." And he wrote to Carlyle that he was "not a poet, but a lover of poetry and poets" — a sort of harbinger of the poets to come.

Emerson's influence was always exerted in the line of the loftiest aspirations. Consequently he will always be dear to thinkers and to poets, and an inspiration to the young. His whole life, however closely examined, shows no flaw of temper or of foible. It was serene and lovely to the end.

NATHAN HASKELL DOLE.

POEMS.

—◆◆◆—

THE SPHYNX.

THE Sphynx is drowsy,
Her wings are furled,
Her ear is heavy,
She broods on the world. —
"Who'll tell me my secret
The ages have kept?
— I awaited the seer,
While they slumbered and slept; —

The fate of the manchild,
The meaning of man;
Known fruit of the unknown,
Dædalian plan;
Out of sleeping a waking,
Out of waking a sleep,
Life death overtaking,
Deep underneath deep.

1

Erect as a sunbeam
Upspringeth the palm;
The elephant browses
Undaunted and calm;
In beautiful motion
The thrush plies his wings;
Kind leaves of his covert!
Your silence he sings.

The waves unashamed
In difference sweet,
Play glad with the breezes,
Old playfellows meet.
The journeying atoms,
Primordial wholes,
Firmly draw, firmly drive,
By their animate poles.

Sea, earth, air, sound, silence,
Plant, quadruped, bird,
By one music enchanted,
One deity stirred,
Each the other adorning,
Accompany still;

Night veileth the morning,
The vapor the hill.

The babe by its mother
Lies bathed in joy,
Glide its hours uncounted,
The sun is its toy;
Shines the peace of all being
Without cloud in its eyes,
And the sum of the world
In soft miniature lies.

But man crouches and blushes,
Absconds and conceals,
He creepeth and peepeth,
He palters and steals;
Infirm, melancholy,
Jealous glancing around,
An oaf, an accomplice,
He poisons the ground.

Out spoke the great mother
Beholding his fear,
At the sound of her accents
Cold shuddered the sphere; —

Who has drugged my boy's cup,
Who has mixed my boy's bread?
Who with sadness and madness
Has turned the manchild's head?"—

I heard a poet answer
Aloud and cheerfully,
"Say on, sweet Sphynx! thy dirges
Are pleasant songs to me.
Deep love lieth under
These pictures of time,
They fade in the light of
Their meaning sublime.

The fiend that man harries,
Is love of the Best;
Yawns the Pit of the Dragon
Lit by rays from the Blest.
The Lethe of Nature
Can't trance him again,
Whose soul sees the Perfect,
Which his eyes seek in vain.

Profounder, profounder,
Man's spirit must dive;

To his aye-rolling orbit
No goal will arrive.
The. heavens that draw him
With sweetness untold,
Once found, — for new heavens
He spurneth the old.

Pride ruined the angels,
Their shame them restores,
And the joy that is sweetest
Lurks in stings of remorse.
Have I a lover
Who is noble and free, —
I would he were nobler
Than to love me.

Eterne alternation
Now follows, now flies,
And under pain, pleasure,
Under pleasure, pain lies.
Love works at the centre,
Heart-heaving alway;
Forth speed the strong pulses
To the borders of day.

Dull Sphynx, Jove keep thy five wits!
Thy sight is growing blear,
Rue, myrrh, and cummin for the Sphynx,
Her muddy eyes to clear."
The old Sphynx bit her thick lip, —
"Who taught thee me to name?
I am thy spirit, yoke-fellow!
Of thine eye I am eyebeam.

Thou art the unanswered question;
Couldst see thy proper eye,
Alway it asketh, asketh,
And each answer is a lie.
So take thy quest through nature,
It through thousand natures ply,
Ask on, thou clothed eternity, —
Time is the false reply."

Uprose the merry Sphynx,
And crouched no more in stone,
She melted into purple cloud,
She silvered in the moon,
She spired into a yellow flame,
She flowered in blossoms red,

She flowed into a foaming wave,
She stood Monadnoc's head.

Thorough a thousand voices
Spoke the universal dame,
"Who telleth one of my meanings,
Is master of all I am."

EACH AND ALL.

Little thinks, in the field, yon red-cloaked
    clown,
Of thee, from the hill-top looking down;
And the heifer, that lows in the upland farm,
Far-heard, lows not thine ear to charm;
The sexton tolling the bell at noon,
Dreams not that great Napoleon
Stops his horse, and lists with delight,
Whilst his files sweep round yon Alpine height;
Nor knowest thou what argument
Thy life to thy neighbor's creed has lent:
All are needed by each one,
Nothing is fair or good alone.

I thought the sparrow's note from heaven,
Singing at dawn on the alder bough;
I brought him home in his nest at even; —
He sings the song, but it pleases not now;
For I did not bring home the river and sky;
He sang to my ear; they sang to my eye.

The delicate shells lay on the shore;
The bubbles of the latest wave
Fresh pearls to their enamel gave;
And the bellowing of the savage sea
Greeted their safe escape to me;
I wiped away the weeds and foam,
And fetched my sea-born treasures home;
But the poor, unsightly, noisome things
Had left their beauty on the shore
With the sun, and the sand, and the wild
    uproar.

The lover watched his graceful maid
As 'mid the virgin train she strayed,
Nor knew her beauty's best attire
Was woven still by the snow-white quire;
At last she came to his hermitage,
Like the bird from the woodlands to the
    cage, —
The gay enchantment was undone,
A gentle wife, but fairy none.

Then I said, "I covet Truth;
Beauty is unripe childhood's cheat, —

I leave it behind with the games of youth."
As I spoke, beneath my feet
The ground-pine curled its pretty wreath,
Running over the club-moss burrs;
I inhaled the violet's breath;
Around me stood the oaks and firs;
Pine cones and acorns lay on the ground;
Above me soared the eternal sky,
Full of light and deity;
Again I saw, again I heard,
The rolling river, the morning bird;—
Beauty through my senses stole,
I yielded myself to the perfect whole.

THE PROBLEM.

I LIKE a church, I like a cowl,
I love a prophet of the soul,
And on my heart monastic aisles
Fall like sweet strains or pensive smiles;
Yet not for all his faith can see,
Would I that cowled churchman be.
Why should the vest on him allure,
Which I could not on me endure?

Not from a vain or shallow thought
His awful Jove young Phidias brought;
Never from lips of cunning fell
The thrilling Delphic oracle;
Out from the heart of nature rolled
The burdens of the Bible old;
The litanies of nations came,
Like the volcano's tongue of flame,
Up from the burning core below,
The canticles of love and woe.

11

The hand that rounded Peter's dome,
And groined the aisles of Christian Rome,
Wrought in a sad sincerity,
Himself from God he could not free;
He builded better than he knew,
The conscious stone to beauty grew.

Know'st thou what wove yon woodbird's
    nest
Of leaves and feathers from her breast;
Or how the fish outbuilt its shell,
Painting with morn each annual cell;
Or how the sacred pine tree adds
To her old leaves new myriads?
Such and so grew these holy piles,
Whilst love and terror laid the tiles.
Earth proudly wears the Parthenon
As the best gem upon her zone;
And Morning opes with haste her lids
To gaze upon the Pyramids;
O'er England's abbeys bends the sky
As on its friends with kindred eye;
For out of Thought's interior sphere
These wonders rose to upper air,

And nature gladly gave them place,
Adopted them into her race,
And granted them an equal date
With Andes and with Ararat.

These temples grew as grows the grass,
Art might obey but not surpass.
The passive Master lent his hand
To the vast soul that o'er him planned,
And the same power that reared the shrine,
Bestrode the tribes that knelt within.
Even the fiery Pentecost
Girds with one flame the Countless host,
Trances the heart through chanting quires,
And through the priest the mind inspires.

The word unto the prophet spoken
Was writ on tables yet unbroken;
The word by seers or sibyls told
In groves of oak, or fanes of gold,
Still floats upon the morning wind,
Still whispers to the willing mind.
One accent of the Holy Ghost
The heedless world hath never lost.

I know what say the Fathers wise,
The Book itself before me lies,
Old *Chrysostom*, best Augustine,
And he who blent both in his line,
The younger *Golden-lips* or mines,
Taylor, the Shakspeare of divines,
His words are music in my ear,
I see his cowled portrait dear,
And yet for all his faith could see,
I would not the good bishop be.

TO RHEA.

Thee, dear friend, a brother soothes,
Not with flatteries, but truths,
Which tarnish not, but purify
To light which dims the morning's eye.
I have come from the spring-woods,
From the fragrant solitudes;
Listen what the poplar tree,
And murmuring waters counselled me.

If with love thy heart has burned,
If thy love is unreturned,
Hide thy grief within thy breast,
Though it tear thee unexpressed.
For, when love has once departed
From the eyes of the false-hearted,
And one by one has torn off quite
The bandages of purple light,
Though thou wert the loveliest
Form the Soul had ever drest,

Thou shalt seem in each reply
A vixen to his altered eye;
Thy softest pleadings seem too bold,
Thy praying lute shall seem to scold.
Though thou kept the straightest road,
Yet thou errest far and broad.

But thou shalt do as do the gods
In their cloudless periods:
For of this lore be thou sure,
Though thou forget, the gods secure
Forget never their command,
But make the statute of this land:
As they lead, so follow all,
Ever have done, ever shall.
Warning to the blind and deaf,
'Tis written on the iron leaf,
Who drinks of Cupid's nectar cup
Loveth downward and not up;
Therefore who loves, of gods or men,
Shall not by the same be loved again;
His sweetheart's idolatry
Falls in turn a new degree.

When a god is once beguiled
By beauty of a mortal child,
And by her radiant youth delighted,
He is not fooled, but warily knoweth,
His love shall never be requited;
And thus the wise Immortal doeth.
'Tis his study and delight
To bless that creature, day and night,
From all evils to defend her,
In her lap to pour all splendor,
To ransack earth for riches rare,
And fetch her stars to deck her hair;
He mixes music with her thoughts,
And saddens her with heavenly doubts;
All grace, all good his great heart knows,
Profuse in love the king bestows,
Saying, Hearken, Earth! Sea! Air!
This monument of my despair
Build I to the All-Good, All-Fair.
Not for a private good,
But I from my beatitude,
Albeit scorned as none was scorned,
Adorn her as was none adorned.
I make this maiden an ensample

To nature through her kingdoms ample,
Whereby to model newer races,
Statelier forms, and fairer faces,
To carry man to new degrees
Of power, and of comeliness.
These presents be the hostages
Which I pawn for my release;
See to thyself, O universe!
Thou art better and not worse. —
And the god having given all,
Is freed forever from his thrall.

THE VISIT.

Askest, "How long thou shalt stay?"
Devastator of the day!
Know, each substance and relation
Thorough nature's operation,
Hath its unit, bound, and metre,
And every new compound
Is some product and repeater,
Product of the early found.
But the unit of the visit,
The encounter of the wise,
Say what other metre is it
Than the meeting of the eyes?
Nature poureth into nature
Through the channels of that feature.
Riding on the ray of Sight,
More fleet than waves or whirlwinds go,
Or for service or delight,
Hearts to hearts their meaning show,

Sum their long experience,
And import intelligence.
Single look has drained the breast,
Single moment years confessed.
The duration of a glance
Is the term of convenance,
And, though thy rede be church or state,
Frugal multiples of that.
Speeding Saturn cannot halt;
Linger, — thou shalt rue the fault,
If Love his moment overstay,
Hatred's swift repulsions play.

URIEL.

IT fell in the ancient periods
Which the brooding soul surveys,
Or ever the wild Time coined itself
Into calendar months and days.

This was the lapse of Uriel,
Which in Paradise befell.
Once among the Pleiads walking,
SAID overheard the young gods talking,
And the treason too long pent
To his ears was evident.
The young deities discussed
Laws of form and metre just,
Orb, quintessence, and sunbeams,
What subsisteth, and what seems.
One, with low tones that decide,
And doubt and reverend use defied,
With a look that solved the sphere,
And stirred the devils everywhere,

Gave his sentiment divine
Against the being of a line:
"Line in nature is not found,
Unit and universe are round;
In vain produced, all rays return,
Evil will bless, and ice will burn."
As Uriel spoke with piercing eye,
A shudder ran around the sky;
The stern old war-gods shook their heads,
The seraphs frowned from myrtle-beds;
Seemed to the holy festival,
The rash word boded ill to all;
The balance-beam of Fate was bent;
The bonds of good and ill were rent;
Strong Hades could not keep his own,
But all slid to confusion.

A sad self-knowledge withering fell
On the beauty of Uriel.
In heaven once eminent, the god
Withdrew that hour into his cloud,
Whether doomed to long gyration
In the sea of generation,
Or by knowledge grown too bright

To hit the nerve of feebler sight.
Straightway a forgetting wind
Stole over the celestial kind,
And their lips the secret kept,
If in ashes the fibre-seed slept.
But now and then truth-speaking things
Shamed the angels' veiling wings,
And, shrilling from the solar course,
Or from fruit of chemic force,
Procession of a soul in matter,
Or the speeding change of water,
Or out of the good of evil born,
Came Uriel's voice of cherub scorn;
And a blush tinged the upper sky,
And the gods shook, they knew not why.

THE WORLD-SOUL.

THANKS to the morning light,
Thanks to the seething sea,
To the uplands of New Hampshire,
To the green-haired forest free;
Thanks to each man of courage,
To the maids of holy mind,
To the boy with his games undaunted,
Who never looks behind.
Cities of proud hotels,
Houses of rich and great,
Vice nestles in your chambers,
Beneath your roofs of slate.
It cannot conquer folly,
Time-and-space-conquering steam, —
And the light-outspeeding telegraph
Bears nothing on its beam.

The politics are base,
The letters do not cheer,

And 'tis far in the deeps of history —
The voice that speaketh clear.
Trade and the streets ensnare us,
Our bodies are weak and worn,
We plot and corrupt each other,
And we despoil the unborn.

Yet there in the parlor sits
Some figure of noble guise,
Our angel in a stranger's form,
Or woman's pleading eyes;
Or only a flashing sunbeam
In at the window pane;
Or music pours on mortals
Its beautiful disdain.

The inevitable morning
Finds them who in cellars be,
And be sure the all-loving Nature
Will smile in a factory.
Yon ridge of purple landscape,
Yon sky between the walls,
Hold all the hidden wonders
In scanty intervals.

Alas, the sprite that haunts us
Deceives our rash desire,
It whispers of the glorious gods,
And leaves us in the mire:
We cannot learn the cipher
That's writ upon our cell,
Stars help us by a mystery
Which we could never spell.

If but one hero knew it,
The world would blush in flame,
The sage, till he hit the secret,
Would hang his head for shame.
But our brothers have not read it,
Not one has found the key,
And henceforth we are comforted,
We are but such as they.

Still, still the secret presses,
The nearing clouds draw down,
The crimson morning flames into
The fopperies of the town.
Within, without, the idle earth
Stars weave eternal rings,

The sun himself shines heartily,
And shares the joy he brings.

And what if trade sow cities
Like shells along the shore,
And thatch with towns the prairie broad
With railways ironed o'er; —
They are but sailing foambells
Along Thought's causing stream,
And take their shape and Sun-color
From him that sends the dream.

For destiny does not like
To yield to men the helm,
And shoots his thought by hidden nerves
Throughout the solid realm.
The patient Dæmon sits
With roses and a shroud,
He has his way, and deals his gifts —
But ours is not allowed.

He is no churl or trifler,
And his viceroy is none,
Love-without-weakness,
Of genius sire and son;

And his will is not thwarted, —
The seeds of land and sea
Are the atoms of his body bright,
And his behest obey.

He serveth the servant,
The brave he loves amain,
He kills the cripple and the sick,
And straight begins again;
For gods delight in gods,
And thrust the weak aside;
To him who scorns their charities,
Their arms fly open wide.

When the old world is sterile,
And the ages are effete,
He will from wrecks and sediment
The fairer world complete.
He forbids to despair,
His cheeks mantle with mirth,
And the unimagined good of men
Is yeaning at the birth.

Spring still makes spring in the mind,
When sixty years are told;

Love wakes anew this throbbing heart,
And we are never old.
Over the winter glaciers,
I see the summer glow,
And through the wild-piled snowdrift
The warm rose buds below.

ALPHONSO OF CASTILE.

I ALPHONSO live and learn,
Seeing nature go astern.
Things deteriorate in kind,
Lemons run to leaves and rind,
Meagre crop of figs and limes,
Shorter days and harder times.
Flowering April cools and dies
In the insufficient skies;
Imps at high Midsummer blot
Half the sun's disk with a spot;
'Twill not now avail to tan
Orange cheek, or skin of man:
Roses bleach, the goats are dry,
Lisbon quakes, the people cry.
Yon pale scrawny fisher fools,
Gaunt as bitterns in the pools,
Are no brothers of my blood, —
They discredit Adamhood.

Eyes of gods! ye must have seen,
O'er your ramparts as ye lean,
The general debility,
Of genius the sterility,
Mighty projects countermanded,
Rash ambition broken-handed,
Puny man and scentless rose
Tormenting Pan to double the dose.
Rebuild or ruin: either fill
Of vital force the wasted rill,
Or, tumble all again in heap
To weltering chaos, and to sleep.

Say, Seigneurs, are the old Niles dry,
Which fed the veins of earth and sky,
That mortals miss the loyal heats
Which drove them erst to social feats,
Now to a savage selfness grown,
Think nature barely serves for one;
With science poorly mask their hurt,
And vex the gods with question pert,
Immensely curious whether you
Still are rulers, or Mildew.

Masters, I'm in pain with you;
Masters, I'll be plain with you.
In my palace of Castile,
I, a king, for kings can feel;
There my thoughts the matter roll,
And solve and oft resolve the whole,
And, for I'm styled Alphonse the Wise,
Ye shall not fail for sound advice,
Before ye want a drop of rain,
Hear the sentiment of Spain.

You have tried famine: no more try it;
Ply us now with a full diet;
Teach your pupils now with plenty,
For one sun supply us twenty:
I have thought it thoroughly over,
State of hermit, state of lover;
We must have society,
We cannot spare variety.
Hear you, then, celestial fellows!
Fits not to be over zealous;
Steads not to work on the clean jump,
Nor wine nor brains perpetual pump;

Men and gods are too extense, —
Could you slacken and condense?
Your rank overgrowths reduce,
Till your kinds abound with juice;
Earth crowded cries, "Too many men," —
My counsel is, Kill nine in ten,
And bestow the shares of all
On the remnant decimal.
Add their nine lives to this cat;
Stuff their nine brains in his hat;
Make his frame and forces square
With the labors he must dare;
Thatch his flesh, and even his years
With the marble which he rears;
There growing slowly old at ease,
No faster than his planted trees,
He may, by warrant of his age,
In schemes of broader scope engage:
So shall ye have a man of the sphere,
Fit to grace the solar year.

MITHRIDATES.

I CANNOT spare water or wine,
Tobacco-leaf, or poppy, or rose;
From the earth-poles to the Line,
All between that works or grows,
Every thing is kin of mine.

Give me agates for my meat,
Give me cantharids to eat,
From air and ocean bring me foods,
From all zones and altitudes.

From all natures, sharp and slimy,
Salt and basalt, wild and tame,
Tree, and lichen, ape, sea-lion,
Bird and reptile be my game.

Ivy for my fillet band,
Blinding dogwood in my hand,

Hemlock for my sherbet cull me,
And the prussic juice to lull me,
Swing me in the upas boughs,
Vampire-fanned, when I carouse.

Too long shut in strait and few,
Thinly dieted on dew,
I will use the world, and sift it,
To a thousand humors shift it,
As you spin a cherry.
O doleful ghosts, and goblins merry,
O all you virtues, methods, mights;
Means, appliances, delights;
Reputed wrongs, and braggart rights;
Smug routine, and things allowed;
Minorities, things under cloud!
Hither! take me, use me, fill me,
Vein and artery, though ye kill me;
God! I will not be an owl,
But sun me in the Capitol.

TO J. W.

Set not thy foot on graves;
Hear what wine and roses say;
The mountain chase, the summer waves,
The crowded town, thy feet may well delay.

Set not thy foot on graves;
Nor seek to unwind the shroud
Which charitable time
And nature have allowed
To wrap the errors of a sage sublime.

Set not thy foot on graves;
Care not to strip the dead
Of his sad ornament;
His myrrh, and wine, and rings,
His sheet of lead,
And trophies buried;
Go get them where he earned them when alive,
As resolutely dig or dive.

Life is too short to waste
The critic bite or cynic bark,
Quarrel, or reprimand;
'Twill soon be dark;
Up! mind thine own aim, and
God speed the mark.

FATE.

THAT you are fair or wise is vain,
Or strong, or rich, or generous;
You must have also the untaught strain
That sheds beauty on the rose.
There is a melody born of melody,
Which melts the world into a sea.
Toil could never compass it,
Art its height could never hit,
It came never out of wit,
But a music music-born
Well may Jove and Juno scorn.
Thy beauty, if it lack the fire
Which drives me mad with sweet desire,
What boots it? what the soldier's mail,
Unless he conquer and prevail?
What all the goods thy pride which lift,
If thou pine for another's gift?
Alas! that one is born in blight,
Victim of perpetual slight; —

When thou lookest in his face,
Thy heart saith, Brother! go thy ways!
None shall ask thee what thou doest,
Or care a rush for what thou knowest,
Or listen when thou repliest,
Or remember where thou liest,
Or how thy supper is sodden, —
And another is born
To make the sun forgotten.
Surely he carries a talisman
Under his tongue;
Broad are his shoulders, and strong,
And his eye is scornful,
Threatening, and young.
I hold it of little matter,
Whether your jewel be of pure water,
A rose diamond or a white, —
But whether it dazzle me with light.
I care not how you are drest,
In the coarsest, or in the best,
Nor whether your name is base or brave,
Nor for the fashion of your behavior, —
But whether you charm me,
Bid my bread feed, and my fire warm me,

And dress up nature in your favor.
One thing is forever good,
That one thing is success, —
Dear to the Eumenides,
And to all the heavenly brood.
Who bides at home, nor looks abroad,
Carries the eagles, and masters the sword.

GUY.

MORTAL mixed of middle clay,
Attempered to the night and day,
Interchangeable with things,
Needs no amulets nor rings.
Guy possessed the talisman
That all things from him began,
And as, of old, Polycrates
Chained the sunshine and the breeze,
So did Guy betimes discover
Fortune was his guard and lover;
In strange junctures, felt with awe
His own symmetry with law,
That no mixture could withstand
The virtue of his lucky hand.
He gold or jewel could not lose,
Nor not receive his ample dues;
In the street, if he turned round,
His eye the eye 'twas seeking found.
It seemed his Genius discreet
Worked on the Maker's own receipt,

41

And made each tide and element
Stewards of stipend and of rent;
So that the common waters fell
As costly wine into his well.
He had so sped his wise affairs
That he caught nature in his snares;
Early or late, the falling rain
Arrived in time to swell his grain;
Stream could not so perversely wind,
But corn of Guy's was there to grind;
The whirlwind found it on its way
To speed his sails, to dry his hay;
And the world's sun seemed to rise
To drudge all day for Guy the wise.
In his rich nurseries, timely skill
Strong crab with nobler blood did fill;
The Zephyr in his garden rolled
From plum trees vegetable gold;
And all the hours of the year
With their own harvest hovered were:
There was no frost but welcome came,
Nor freshet, nor midsummer flame;
Belonged to wind and world the toil
And venture, and to Guy the oil.

TACT.

WHAT boots it, thy virtue,
What profit thy parts,
While one thing thou lackest,
The art of all arts!
The only credentials,
Passport to success,
Opens castle and parlor, —
Address, man, Address.

The maiden in danger
Was saved by the swain,
His stout arm restored her
To Broadway again:

The maid would reward him, —
Gay company come, —
They laugh, she laughs with them,
He is moonstruck and dumb.

This clenches the bargain,
Sails out of the bay,
Gets the vote in the Senate,
Spite of Webster and Clay;

Has for genius no mercy,
For speeches no heed, —
It lurks in the eyebeam,
It leaps to its deed.

Church, tavern, and market,
Bed and board it will sway;
It has no to-morrow,
It ends with to-day.

HAMATREYA.

Minott, Lee, Willard, Hosmer, Meriam, Flint,
Possessed the land, which rendered to their
toil
Hay, corn, roots, hemp, flax, apples, wool,
and wood.
Each of these landlords walked amidst his
farm,
Saying, "'Tis mine, my children's, and my
name's.
How sweet the west wind sounds in my own
trees;
How graceful climb those shadows on my hill;
I fancy those pure waters and the flags
Know me as does my dog: we sympathize,
And, I affirm, my actions smack of the soil."
Where are those men? Asleep beneath their
grounds,
And strangers, fond as they, their furrows
plough.

Earth laughs in flowers to see her boastful boys
Earth proud, proud of the earth which is not
    theirs;
Who steer the plough, but cannot steer their
    feet
Clear of the grave. —
They added ridge to valley, brook to pond,
And sighed for all that bounded their domain,
"This suits me for a pasture; that's my park,
We must have clay, lime, gravel, granite-ledge,
And misty lowland where to go for peat.
The land is well, — lies fairly to the south.
'Tis good, when you have crossed the sea and
    back,
To find the sitfast acres where you left them."
Ah! the hot owner sees not Death, who adds
Him to his land, a lump of mould the more.
Hear what the Earth says:

EARTH-SONG.

    Mine and yours,
    Mine not yours.
    Earth endures,
    Stars abide,

Shine down in the old sea,
Old are the shores,
But where are old men?
I who have seen much,
Such have I never seen.
The lawyer's deed
Ran sure
In tail
To them and to their heirs
Who shall succeed
Without fail
For evermore.

Here is the land,
Shaggy with wood,
With its old valley,
Mound, and flood. —
But the heritors —
Fled like the flood's foam;
The lawyer, and the laws,
And the kingdom,
Clean swept herefrom.

They called me theirs,
Who so controlled me;

Yet every one
Wished to stay, and is gone.
How am I theirs,
If they cannot hold me,
But I hold them?

When I- heard the Earth-song,
I was no longer brave;
My avarice cooled
Like lust in the chill of the grave.

GOOD-BY.

Good-by, proud world, I'm going home,
Thou'rt not my friend, and I'm not thine;
Long through thy weary crowds I roam;
A river-ark on the ocean brine,
Long I've been tossed like the driven foam,
. But now, proud world, I'm going home.

Good-by to Flattery's fawning face,
To Grandeur, with his wise grimace,
To upstart Wealth's averted eye,
To supple Office low and high,
To crowded halls, to court, and street,
To frozen hearts, and hasting feet,
To those who go, and those who come,
Good-by, proud world, I'm going home.

I'm going to my own hearth-stone
Bosomed in yon green hills, alone,
A secret nook in a pleasant land,
Whose groves the frolic fairies planned;

49

Where arches green the livelong day
Echo the blackbird's roundelay,
And vulgar feet have never trod
A spot that is sacred to thought and God.

Oh, when I am safe in my sylvan home,
I tread on the pride of Greece and Rome;
And when I am stretched beneath the pines
Where the evening star so holy shines,
I laugh at the lore and the pride of man,
At the sophist schools, and the learned clan;
For what are they all in their high conceit,
When man in the bush with God may meet.

THE RHODORA,

ON BEING ASKED, WHENCE IS THE FLOWER.

In May, when sea-winds pierced our solitudes,
I found the fresh Rhodora in the woods,
Spreading its leafless blooms in a damp nook,
To please the desert and the sluggish brook.
The purple petals fallen in the pool
Made the black water with their beauty gay;
Here might the red-bird come his plumes to cool,
And court the flower that cheapens his array.
Rhodora! if the sages ask thee why
This charm is wasted on the earth and sky,
Tell them, dear, that, if eyes were made for
    seeing,
Then beauty is its own excuse for being;
Why thou wert there, O rival of the rose!
I never thought to ask; I never knew;
But in my simple ignorance suppose
The self-same power that brought me there,
    brought you.

THE HUMBLEBEE.

BURLY dozing humblebee!
Where thou art is clime for me.
Let them sail for Porto Rique,
Far-off heats through seas to seek,
I will follow thee alone,
Thou animated torrid zone!
Zig-zag steerer, desert-cheerer,
Let me chase thy waving lines,
Keep me nearer, me thy hearer,
Singing over shrubs and vines.

Insect lover of the sun,
Joy of thy dominion!
Sailor of the atmosphere,
Swimmer through the waves of air,
Voyager of light and noon,
Epicurean of June,
Wait I prithee, till I come
Within ear-shot of thy hum, —
All without is martyrdom.

When the south wind, in May days,
With a net of shining haze,
Silvers the horizon wall,
And, with softness touching all,
Tints the human countenance
With a color of romance,
And, infusing subtle heats,
Turns the sod to violets,
Thou in sunny solitudes,
Rover of the underwoods,
The green silence dost displace,
With thy mellow breezy bass.

Hot midsummer's petted crone,
Sweet to me thy drowsy tune,
Telling of countless sunny hours,
Long days, and solid banks of flowers,
Of gulfs of sweetness without bound
In Indian wildernesses found,
Of Syrian peace, immortal leisure,
Firmest cheer and bird-like pleasure.

Aught unsavory or unclean,
Hath my insect never seen,

But violets and bilberry bells,
Maple sap and daffodels,
Grass with green flag half-mast high,
Succory to match the sky,
Columbine with horn of honey,
Scented fern, and agrimony,
Clover, catchfly, adders-tongue,
And brier-roses dwelt among;
All beside was unknown waste,
All was picture as he passed.

Wiser far than human seer,
Yellow-breeched philosopher!
Seeing only what is fair,
Sipping only what is sweet,
Thou dost mock at fate and care,
Leave the chaff and take the wheat.
When the fierce north-western blast
Cools sea and land so far and fast,
Thou already slumberest deep, —
Woe and want thou canst out-sleep, —
Want and woe which torture us,
Thy sleep makes ridiculous.

BERRYING.

"MAY be true what I had heard,
Earth's a howling wilderness
Truculent with fraud and force,"
Said I, strolling through the pastures,
And along the riverside.
Caught among the blackberry vines,
Feeding on the Ethiops sweet,
Pleasant fancies overtook me:
I said, "What influence me preferred
Elect to dreams thus beautiful?"
The vines replied, "And didst thou deem
No wisdom to our berries went?"

THE SNOW-STORM.

ANNOUNCED by all the trumpets of the sky
Arrives the snow, and, driving o'er the fields,
Seems nowhere to alight: the whited air
Hides hills and woods, the river and the
    heaven,
And veils the farm-house at the garden's end.
The steed and traveller stopped, the courier's
    feet
Delayed, all friends shut out, the housemates
    sit
Around the radiant fireplace, enclosed
In a tumultuous privacy of storm.

       Come, see the north wind's masonry.
Out of an unseen quarry evermore
Furnished with tile, the fierce artificer
Curves his white bastions with projected roof
Round every windward stake, or tree, or door.
Speeding, the myriad-handed, his wild work

So fanciful, so savage, naught cares he
For number or proportion.   Mockingly
On coop or kennel he hangs Parian wreaths;
A swan-like form invests the hidden thorn;
Fills up the farmer's lane from wall to wall,
Maugre the farmer's sighs, and at the gate
A tapering turret overtops the work.
And when his hours are numbered, and the
    world
Is all his own, retiring, as he were not,
Leaves, when the sun appears, astonished Art
To mimic in slow structures, stone by stone
Built in an age, the mad wind's night-work,
The frolic architecture of the snow.

WOOD NOTES.

I.

FOR this present, hard
Is the fortune of the bard
Born out of time;
All his accomplishment
From nature's utmost treasure spent
Booteth not him.
When the pine tosses its cones
To the song of its waterfall tones,
He speeds to the woodland walks,
To birds and trees he talks.
Cæsar of his leafy Rome,
There the poet is at home.
He goes to the riverside, —
Not hook nor line hath he:
He stands in the meadows wide, —
Nor gun nor scythe to see;
With none has he to do,
And none seek him,

Nor men below,
Nor spirits dim.
Sure some god his eye enchants,
What he knows, nobody wants.
In the wood he travels glad
Without better fortune had,
Melancholy without bad.
Planter of celestial plants,
What he knows, nobody wants, —
What he knows, he hides, not vaunts.
Knowledge this man prizes best
Seems fantastic to the rest,
Pondering shadows, colors, clouds,
Grass buds, and caterpillars' shrouds,
Boughs on which the wild bees settle,
Tints that spot the violet's petal,
Why nature loves the number five,
And why the star-form she repeats,
Lover of all things alive,
Wonderer at all he meets,
Wonderer chiefly at himself, —
Who can tell him what he is,
Or how meet in human elf
Coming and past eternities?

2.

And such I knew, a forest seer,
A minstrel of the natural year,
Foreteller of the vernal ides,
Wise harbinger of spheres and tides,
A lover true who knew by heart
Each joy the mountain dales impart;
It seemed that nature could not raise
A plant in any secret place,
In quaking bog, on snowy hill,
Beneath the grass that shades the rill,
Under the snow, between the rocks,
In damp fields known to bird and fox,
But he would come in the very hour
It opened in its virgin bower,
As if a sunbeam showed the place,
And tell its long-descended race.
It seemed as if the breezes brought him,
It seemed as if the sparrows taught him,
As if by secret sight he knew
Where in far fields the orchis grew.
There are many events in the field
Which are not shown to common eyes,

But all her shows did nature yield
. To please and win this pilgrim wise.
He saw the partridge drum in the woods,
He heard the woodcock's evening hymn,
He found the tawny thrush's broods,
And the shy hawk did wait for him.
What others did at distance hear,
And guessed within the thicket's gloom,
Was showed to this philosopher,
And at his bidding seemed to come.

3.

In unploughed Maine, he sought the lum-
    berer's gang,
Where from a hundred lakes young rivers
    sprang;
He trod the unplanted forest-floor, whereon
The all-seeing sun for ages hath not shone,
Where feeds the mouse, and walks the surly
    bear,
And up the tall mast runs the woodpecker.
He saw, beneath dim aisles, in odorous beds,
The slight Linnæa hang its twin-born heads,

And blessed the monument of the man of
    flowers,
Which breathes his sweet fame through the
    Northern bowers.
He heard when in the grove, at intervals,
With sudden roar the aged pine tree falls, —
One crash the death-hymn of the perfect
    tree,
Declares the close of its green century.
Low lies the plant to whose creation went
Sweet influence from every element;
Whose living towers the years conspired to
    build,
Whose giddy top the morning loved to gild.
Through these green tents, by eldest nature
    drest,
He roamed, content alike with man and beast.
Where darkness found him, he lay glad at
    night;
There the red morning touched him with its
    light.
Three moons his great heart him a hermit
    made,
So long he roved at will the boundless shade.

The timid it concerns to ask their way,
And fear what foe in caves and swamps can
    stray,
To make no step until the event is known,
And ills to come as evils past bemoan:
Not so the wise; no coward watch he keeps,
To spy what danger on his pathway creeps;
Go where he will, the wise man is at home,
His hearth the earth; — his hall the azure
    dome;
Where his clear spirit leads him, there's his
    road,
By God's own light illumined and foreshowed.

4.

'Twas one of the charmed days
When the genius of God doth flow,
The wind may alter twenty ways,
A tempest cannot blow:
It may blow north, it still is warm;
Or south, it still is clear;
Or east, it smells like a clover farm;
Or west, no thunder fear.

The musing peasant lowly great
Beside the forest water sate:
The rope-like pine-roots crosswise grown
Composed the network of his throne;
The wide lake edged with sand and grass
Was burnished to a floor of glass,
Painted with shadows green and proud
Of the tree and of the cloud.
He was the heart of all the scene,
On him the sun looked more serene,
To hill and cloud his face was known,
It seemed the likeness of their own.
They knew by secret sympathy
The public child of earth and sky.
You ask, he said, what guide,
Me through trackless thickets led,
Through thick-stemmed woodlands rough and
    wide?
I found the waters' bed:
I travelled grateful by their side,
Or through their channel dry;
They led me through the thicket damp,
Through brake and fern, the beavers' camp,
Through beds of granite cut my road,

And their resistless friendship showed.
The falling waters led me,
The foodful waters fed me,
And brought me to the lowest land,
Unerring to the ocean sand.
The moss upon the forest bark
Was pole-star when the night was dark;
The purple berries in the wood
Supplied me necessary food.
For nature ever faithful is
To such as trust her faithfulness.
When the forest shall mislead me,
When the night and morning lie,
When sea and land refuse to feed me,
'Twill be time enough to die;
Then will yet my mother yield
A pillow in her greenest field,
Nor the June flowers scorn to cover
The clay of their departed lover.

WOOD NOTES.

II.

As sunbeams stream through liberal space,
And nothing jostle or displace,
So waved the pine tree through my thought,
And fanned the dreams it never brought.

"Whether is better the gift or the donor?
Come to me,"
Quoth the pine tree,
"I am the giver of honor.
My garden is the cloven rock,
And my manure the snow,
And drifting sand heaps feed my stock,
In summer's scorching glow.
Ancient or curious,
Who knoweth aught of us?
Old as Jove,
Old as Love,

Who of me
Tells the pedigree?
Only the mountains old,
Only the waters cold,
Only moon and star
My coevals are.
Ere the first fowl sung
My relenting boughs among,
Ere Adam wived,
Ere Adam lived,
Ere the duck dived,
Ere the bees hived,
Ere the lion roared,
Ere the eagle soared,
Light and heat, land and sea
Spake unto the oldest tree.
Glad in the sweet and secret aid
Which matter unto matter paid,
The water flowed, the breezes fanned,
The tree confined the roving sand,
The sunbeam gave me to the sight,
The tree adorned the formless light,
And once again
O'er the grave of men

We shall talk to each other again
Of the old age behind,
Of the time out of mind,
Which shall come again."

"Whether is better the gift or the donor?
Come to me,"
Quoth the pine tree,
"I am the giver of honor.
He is great who can live by me;
The rough and bearded forester
Is better than the lord;
God fills the scrip and canister,
Sin piles the loaded board.
The lord is the peasant that was,
The peasant the lord that shall be,
The lord is hay, the peasant grass,
One dry and one the living tree.
Genius with my boughs shall flourish,
Want and cold our roots shall nourish;
Who liveth by the ragged pine,
Foundeth a heroic line;
Who liveth in the palace hall,
Waneth fast and spendeth all:

He goes to my savage haunts,
With his chariot and his care,
My twilight realm he disenchants,
And finds his prison there.
What prizes the town and the tower?
Only what the pine tree yields,
Sinew that subdued the fields,
The wild-eyed boy who in the woods
Chants his hymn to hill and floods,
Whom the city's poisoning spleen
Made not pale, or fat, or lean,
Whom the rain and the wind purgeth,
Whom the dawn and the day-star urgeth,
In whose cheek the rose leaf blusheth,
In whose feet the lion rusheth,
Iron arms and iron mould,
That knew not fear, fatigue, or cold.
I give my rafters to his boat,
My billets to his boiler's throat,
And I will swim the ancient sea
To float my child to victory,
And grant to dwellers with the pine,
Dominion o'er the palm and vine.
Westward I ope the forest gates,

The train along the railroad skates,
It leaves the land behind, like ages past,
The foreland flows to it in river fast,
Missouri I have made a mart,
I teach Iowa Saxon art.
Who leaves the pine tree, leaves his friend,
Unnerves his strength, invites his end.
Cut a bough from my parent stem,
And dip it in thy porcelain vase;
A little while each russet gem
Will swell and rise with wonted grace,
But when it seeks enlarged supplies,
The orphan of the forest dies.

Whoso walketh in solitude,
And inhabiteth the wood,
Choosing light, wave, rock, and bird,
Before the money-loving herd,
Into that forester shall pass
From these companions power and grace;
Clean shall he be without, within,
From the old adhering sin;
Love shall he, but not adulate,
The all-fair, the all-embracing Fate,

All ill dissolving in the light
Of his triumphant piercing sight.
Not vain, sour, nor frivolous,
Not mad, athirst, nor garrulous,
Grave, chaste, contented, though retired,
And of all other men desired.
On him the light of star and moon
Shall fall with purer radiance down;
All constellations of the sky
Shed their virtue through his eye.
Him nature giveth for defence
His formidable innocence,
The mountain sap, the shells, the sea,
All spheres, all stones, his helpers be;
He shall never be old,
Nor his fate shall be foretold;
He shall see the speeding year,
Without wailing, without fear;
He shall be happy in his love,
Like to like shall joyful prove.
He shall be happy whilst he woos
Muse-born a daughter of the Muse;
But if with gold she bind her hair,
And deck her breast with diamond,

Take off thine eyes, thy heart forbear,
Though thou lie alone on the ground:
The robe of silk in which she shines,
It was woven of many sins,
And the shreds
Which she sheds
In the wearing of the same,
Shall be grief on grief,
And shame on shame.
Heed the old oracles,
Ponder my spells,
Song wakes in my pinnacles,
When the wind swells.
Soundeth the prophetic wind,
The shadows shake on the rock behind,
And the countless leaves of the pine are strings
Tuned to the lay the wood-god sings.
Hearken! hearken!
If thou wouldst know the mystic song
Chanted when the sphere was young,
Aloft, abroad, the pæan swells,
O wise man, hear'st thou half it tells?
O wise man, hear'st thou the least part?
'Tis the chronicle of art.

To the open ear it sings
The early genesis of things;
Of tendency through endless ages,
Of star-dust, and star-pilgrimages,
Of rounded worlds, of space, and time,
Of the old flood's subsiding slime,
Of chemic matter, force, and form,
Of poles and powers, cold, wet, and warm,
The rushing metamorphosis
Dissolving all that fixture is,
Melts things that be to things that seem,
And solid nature to a dream.
Oh, listen to the under song,
The ever old, the ever young,
And far within those cadent pauses,
The chorus of the ancient Causes.
Delights the dreadful destiny
To fling his voice into the tree,
And shock thy weak ear with a note
Breathed from the everlasting throat.
In music he repeats the pang
Whence the fair flock of nature sprang.
O mortal! thy ears are stones;
These echoes are laden with tones

Which only the pure can hear,
Thou canst not catch what they recite
Of Fate, and Will, of Want, and Right,
Of man to come, of human life,
Of Death, and Fortune, Growth, and Strife."

Once again the pine tree sung; —
"Speak not thy speech my boughs among,
Put off thy years, wash in the breeze,
My hours are peaceful centuries.
Talk no more with feeble tongue;
No more the fool of space and time,
Come weave with mine a nobler rhyme.
Only thy Americans
Can read thy line, can meet thy glance,
But the runes that I rehearse
Understands the universe.
The least breath my boughs which tossed
Brings again the Pentecost;
To every soul it soundeth clear
In a voice of solemn cheer,
'Am I not thine? are not these thine?'
And they reply, 'Forever mine.'
My branches speak Italian,

English, German, Basque, Castilian,
Mountain speech to Highlanders,
Ocean tongues to islanders,
To Finn, and Lap, and swart Malay,
To each his bosom secret say.

Come learn with me the fatal song
Which knits the world in music strong,
Whereto every bosom dances
Kindled with courageous fancies:
Come lift thine eyes to lofty rhymes
Of things with things, of times with times,
Primal chimes of sun and shade,
Of sound and echo, man and maid;
The land reflected in the flood;
Body with shadow still pursued.
For nature beats in perfect tune,
And rounds with rhyme her every rune,
Whether she work in land or sea,
Or hide underground her alchemy.
Thou canst not wave thy staff in air,
Or dip thy paddle in the lake,
But it carves the bow of beauty there,
And the ripples in rhymes the oar forsake.

The wood is wiser far than thou:
The wood and wave each other know.
Not unrelated, unaffied,
But to each thought and thing allied,
Is perfect nature's every part,
Rooted in the mighty heart.
But thou, poor child! unbound, unrhymed,
Whence camest thou, misplaced, mistimed?
Whence, O thou orphan and defrauded?
Is thy land peeled, thy realm marauded?
Who thee divorced, deceived, and left;
Thee of thy faith who hath bereft,
And torn the ensigns from thy brow,
And sunk the immortal eye so low?
Thy cheek too white, thy form too slender,
Thy gait too slow, thy habits tender,
For royal man; they thee confess
An exile from the wilderness, —
The hills where health with health agrees,
And the wise soul expels disease.
Hark! in thy ear I will tell the sign
By which thy hurt thou mayst divine.
When thou shalt climb the mountain cliff,
Or see the wide shore from thy skiff,

To thee the horizon shall express
Only emptiness and emptiness;
There is no man of nature's worth
In the circle of the earth,
And to thine eye the vast skies fall
Dire and satirical
On clucking hens, and prating fools,
On thieves, on drudges, and on dolls.
And thou shalt say to the Most High,
'Godhead! all this astronomy,
And Fate, and practice, and invention,
Strong art, and beautiful pretension,
This radiant pomp of sun and star,
Throes that were, and worlds that are,
Behold! were in vain and in vain; —
It cannot be, — I will look again, —
Surely now will the curtain rise,
And earth's fit tenant me surprise;
But the curtain doth *not* rise,
And nature has miscarried wholly
Into failure, into folly.'

Alas! thine is the bankruptcy,
Blessed nature so to see.

Come lay thee in my soothing shade,
And heal the hurts which sin has made.
I will teach the bright parable
Older than time,
Things undeclarable,
Visions sublime.
I see thee in the crowd alone;
I will be thy companion.
Let thy friends be as the dead in doom,
And build to them a final tomb;
Let the starred shade which mighty falls
Still celebrate their funerals,
And the bell of beetle and of bee
Knell their melodious memory.
Behind thee leave thy merchandise,
Thy churches, and thy charities,
And leave thy peacock wit behind;
Enough for thee the primal mind
That flows in streams, that breathes in wind.
Leave all thy pedant lore apart;
God hid the whole world in thy heart.
Love shuns the sage, the child it crowns,
And gives them all who all renounce.
The rain comes when the wind calls,

The river knows the way to the sea,
Without a pilot it runs and falls,
Blessing all lands with its charity.
The sea tosses and foams to find
Its way up to the cloud and wind,
The shadow sits close to the flying ball,
The date fails not on the palm tree tall,
And thou, — go burn thy wormy pages, —
Shalt outsee the seer, outwit the sages.
Oft didst thou thread the woods in vain
To find what bird had piped the strain, —
Seek not, and the little eremite
Flies gayly forth and sings in sight.

Hearken! once more;
I will tell the mundane lore.
Older am I than thy numbers wot,
Change I may, but I pass not;
Hitherto all things fast abide,
And anchored in the tempest ride.
Trendrant time behooves to hurry
All to yean and all to bury;
All the forms are fugitive,
But the substances survive.

Ever fresh the broad creation,
A divine improvisation,
From the heart of God proceeds,
A single will, a million deeds.
Once slept the world an egg of stone,
And pulse, and sound, and light was none;
And God said, Throb; and there was motion,
And the vast mass became vast ocean.
Onward and on, the eternal Pan
Who layeth the world's incessant plan,
Halteth never in one shape,
But forever doth escape,
Like wave or flame, into new forms
Of gem, and air, of plants and worms.
I, that to-day am a pine,
Yesterday was a bundle of grass.
He is free and libertine,
Pouring of his power the wine
To every age, to every race,
Unto every race and age
He emptieth the beverage;
Unto each, and unto all,
Maker and original.
The world is the ring of his spells,

And the play of his miracles.
As he giveth to all to drink,
Thus or thus they are and think.
He giveth little or giveth much,
To make them several or such.
With one drop sheds form and feature,
With the second a special nature,
The third adds heat's indulgent spark,
The fourth gives light which eats the dark.
In the fifth drop himself he flings,
And conscious Law is King of Kings.
Pleaseth him the Eternal Child
To play his sweet will, glad and wild;
As the bee through the garden ranges,
From world to world the godhead changes;
As the sheep go feeding through the waste,
From form to form he maketh haste.
This vault which glows immense with light
Is the inn where he lodges for a night.
What recks such Traveller if the bowers
Which bloom and fade like summer flowers,
A bunch of fragrant lilies be,
Or the stars of eternity?
Alike to him the better, the worse,

The glowing angel, the outcast corse.
Thou metest him by centuries,
And lo! he passes like the breeze;
Thou seek'st in globe and galaxy,
He hides in pure transparency;
Thou askest in fountains and in fires,
He is the essence that inquires.
He is the axis of the star;
He is the sparkle of the spar;
He is the heart of every creature;
He is the meaning of each feature;
And his mind is the sky
Than all it holds more deep, more high."

MONADNOC.

THOUSAND minstrels woke within me,
"Our music's in the hills;"—
Gayest pictures rose to win me,
Leopard-colored rills.
Up!—If thou knew'st who calls
To twilight parks of beech and pine,
High over the river intervals,
Above the ploughman's highest line,
Over the owner's farthest walls;—
Up!—where the airy citadel
O'erlooks the purging landscape's swell.
Let not unto the stones the day
Her lily and rose, her sea and land display;
Read the celestial sign!
Lo! the South answers to the North;
Bookworm, break this sloth urbane;
A greater Spirit bids thee forth,
Than the gray dreams which thee detain.

Mark how the climbing Oreads
Beckon thee to their arcades;
Youth, for a moment free as they,
Teach thy feet to feel the ground,
Ere yet arrive the wintry· day
When Time thy feet has bound.
Accept the bounty of thy birth;
Taste the lordship of the earth.

I heard and I obeyed,
Assured that he who pressed the claim,
Well-known, but loving not a name,
Was not to be gainsaid.

Ere yet the summoning voice was still,
I turned to Cheshire's haughty hill.
From the fixed cone the cloud-rack flowed
Like ample banner flung abroad
Round about, a hundred miles,
With invitation to the sea, and to the border-
ing isles.

In his own loom's garment drest,
By his own bounty blest,

Fast abides this constant giver,
Pouring many a cheerful river;
To far eyes, an aërial isle,
Unploughed, which finer spirits pile,
Which morn and crimson evening paint
For bard, for lover, and for saint;
The country's core,
Inspirer, prophet evermore,
Pillar which God aloft had set
So that men might it not forget,
It should be their life's ornament,
And mix itself with each event;
Their calendar and dial,
Barometer, and chemic phial,
Garden of berries, perch of birds,
Pasture of pool-haunting herds,
Graced by each change of sum untold,
Earth-baking heat, stone-cleaving cold.

The Titan minds his sky-affairs,
Rich rents and wide alliance shares;
Mysteries of color daily laid
By the great sun in light and shade,
And sweet varieties of chance,

And the mystic seasons' dance,
And thief-like step of liberal hours
Which thawed the snow-drift into flowers.
O wondrous craft of plant and stone
By eldest science done and shown!
Happy, I said, whose home is here,
Fair fortunes to the mountaineer!
Boon nature to his poorest shed
Has royal pleasure-grounds outspread.
Intent I searched the region round,
And in low hut my monarch found.
He was no eagle and no earl,
Alas! my foundling was a churl,
With heart of cat, and eyes of bug,
Dull victim of his pipe and mug;
Woe is me for my hopes' downfall!
Lord! is yon squalid peasant all
That this proud nursery could breed
For God's vicegerency and stead?
Time out of mind this forge of ores,
Quarry of spars in mountain pores,
Old cradle, hunting ground, and bier
Of wolf and otter, bear, and deer;
Well-built abode of many a race;

Tower of observance searching space;
Factory of river, and of rain;
Link in the alps' globe-girding chain;
By million changes skilled to tell
What in the Eternal standeth well,
And what obedient nature can, —
Is this colossal talisman
Kindly to creature, blood, and kind,
And speechless to the master's mind?

I thought to find the patriots
In whom the stock of freedom roots.
To myself I oft recount
Tales of many a famous mount. —
Wales, Scotland, Uri, Hungary's dells,
Roys, and Scanderbegs, and Tells.
Here now shall nature crowd her powers,
Her music, and her meteors,
And, lifting man to the blue deep
Where stars their perfect courses keep,
Like wise preceptor lure his eye
To sound the science of the sky,
And carry learning to its height
Of untried power and sane delight;

The Indian cheer, the frosty skies
Breed purer wits, inventive eyes,
Eyes that frame cities where none be,
And hands that stablish what these see:
And, by the moral of his place,
Hint summits of heroic grace;
Man in these crags a fastness find
To fight pollution of the mind;
In the wide thaw and ooze of wrong,
Adhere like this foundation strong,
The insanity of towns to stem
With simpleness for stratagem.
But if the brave old mould is broke,
And end in clowns the mountain-folk,
In tavern cheer and tavern joke, —
Sink, O mountain! in the swamp,
Hide in thy skies, O sovereign lap!
Perish like leaves the highland breed!
No sire survive, no son succeed!

Soft! let not the offended muse
Toil's hard hap with scorn accuse.
Many hamlets sought I then,
Many farms of mountain men; —

Found I not a minstrel seed,
But men of bone, and good at need.
Rallying round a parish steeple
Nestle warm the highland people,
Coarse and boisterous, yet mild,
Strong as giant, slow as child,
Smoking in a squalid room,
Where yet the westland breezes come.
Close hid in those rough guises lurk
Western magians, here they work;
Sweat and season are their arts,
Their talismans are ploughs and carts;
And well the youngest can command
Honey from the frozen land,
With sweet hay the swamp adorn,
Change the running sand to corn,
For wolves and foxes, lowing herds,
And for cold mosses, cream and curds;
Weave wood to canisters and mats,
Drain sweet maple-juice in vats.
No bird is safe that cuts the air,
From their rifle or their snare;
No fish in river or in lake,
But their long hands it thence will take;

And the country's iron face
Like wax their fashioning skill betrays,
To fill the hollows, sink the hills,
Bridge gulfs, drain swamps, build dams and mills,
And fit the bleak and howling place
For gardens of a finer race,
The world-soul knows his own affair,
Fore-looking when his hands prepare
For the next ages men of mould,
Well embodied, well ensouled,
He cools the present's fiery glow,
Sets the life pulse strong, but slow.
Bitter winds and fasts austere.
His quarantines and grottos, where
He slowly cures decrepit flesh,
And brings it infantile and fresh.
These exercises are the toys
And games with which he breathes his boys.
They bide their time, and well can prove,
If need were, their line from Jove,
Of the same stuff, and so allayed,
As that whereof the sun is made;
And of that fibre quick and strong
Whose throbs are love, whose thrills are song.

Now in sordid weeds they sleep,
Their secret now in dulness keep.
Yet, will you learn our ancient speech,
These the masters who can teach,
Fourscore or a hundred words
All their vocal muse affords,
These they turn in other fashion
Than the writer or the parson.
I can spare the college-bell,
And the learned lecture well.
Spare the clergy and libraries,
Institutes and dictionaries,
For the hardy English root
Thrives here unvalued underfoot.
Rude poets of the tavern hearth,
Squandering your unquoted mirth,
Which keeps the ground and never soars,
While Jake retorts and Reuben roars,
Tough and screaming as birch-bark,
Goes like bullet to its mark,
While the solid curse and jeer
Never balk the waiting ear:
To student ears keen-relished jokes
On truck, and stock, and farming-folks, —

Nought the mountain yields thereof
But savage health and sinews tough.

On the summit as I stood,
O'er the wide floor of plain and flood,
Seemed to me the towering hill
Was not altogether still,
But a quiet sense conveyed;
If I err not, thus it said:

Many feet in summer seek
Betimes my far-appearing peak;
In the dreaded winter-time,
None save dappling shadows climb
Under clouds my lonely head,
Old as the sun, old almost as the shade.
And comest thou
To see strange forests and new snow,
And tread uplifted land?
And leavest thou thy lowland race,
Here amid clouds to stand,
And would'st be my companion,
Where I gaze
And shall gaze

When forests fall, and man is gone,
Over tribes and over times
As the burning Lyre
Nearing me,
With its stars of northern fire,
In many a thousand years.

Ah! welcome, if thou bring
My secret in thy brain;
To mountain-top may muse's wing
With good allowance strain.
Gentle pilgrim, if thou know
The gamut old of Pan,
And how the hills began,
The frank blessings of the hill
Fall on thee, as fall they will.
'Tis the law of bush and stone —
Each can only take his own.
Let him heed who can and will, —
Enchantment fixed me here
To stand the hurts of time, until
In mightier chant I disappear.
If thou trowest
How the chemic eddies play

Pole to pole, and what they say,
And that these gray crags
Not on crags are hung,
But beads are of a rosary
On prayer and music strung;
And, credulous, through the granite seeming
Seest the smile of Reason beaming;
Can thy style-discerning eye
The hidden-working Builder spy,
Who builds, yet makes no chips, no din,
With hammer soft as snow-flake's flight;
Knowest thou this?
O pilgrim, wandering not amiss!
Already my rocks lie light,
And soon my cone will spin.
For the world was built in order,
And the atoms march in tune,
Rhyme the pipe, and time the warder,
Cannot forget the sun, the moon.
Orb and atom forth they prance,
When they hear from far the rune,
None so backward in the troop,
When the music and the dance
Reach his place and circumstance,

But knows the sun-creating sound,
And, though a pyramid, will bound.

Monadnoc is a mountain strong,
Tall and good my kind among,
But well I know, no mountain can
Measure with a perfect man;
For it is on Zodiack's writ,
Adamant is soft to wit;
And when the greater comes again,
With my music in his brain,
I shall pass as glides my shadow
Daily over hill and meadow.

Through all time
I hear the approaching feet
Along the flinty pathway beat
Of him that cometh, and shall come, —
Of him who shall as lightly bear
My daily load of woods and streams,
As now the round sky-cleaving boat
Which never strains its rocky beams,
Whose timbers, as they silent float,
Alps and Caucasus uprear,

And the long Alleghanies here,
And all town-sprinkled lands that be,
Sailing through stars with all their history.

Every morn I lift my head,
Gaze o'er New England underspread
South from Saint Lawrence to the Sound,
From Katshill east to the sea-bound.
Anchored fast for many an age,
I await the bard and sage,
Who in large thoughts, like fair pearl-seed,
Shall string Monadnoc like a bead.
Comes that cheerful troubadour,
This mound shall throb his face before,
As when with inward fires and pain
It rose a bubble from the plain.
When he cometh, I shall shed
From this well-spring in my head
Fountain drop of spicier worth
Than all vintage of the earth.
There's fruit upon my barren soil
Costlier far than wine or oil;
There's a berry blue and gold, —
Autumn-ripe its juices hold,

Sparta's stoutness, Bethlehem's heart,
Asia's rancor, Athens' art,
Slowsure Britain's secular might,
And the German's inward sight;
I will give my son to eat
Best of Pan's immortal meat,
Bread to eat and juice to drink,
So the thoughts that he shall think
Shall not be forms of stars, but stars,
Nor pictures pale, but Jove and Mars.

He comes, but not of that race bred
Who daily climb my specular head.
Oft as morning wreathes my scarf,
Fled the last plumule of the dark,
Pants up hither the spruce clerk
From South-Cove and City-wharf;
I take him up my rugged sides,
Half-repentant, scant of breath, —
Bead-eyes my granite chaos show,
And my midsummer snow;
Open the daunting map beneath, —
All his county, sea and land,
Dwarfed to measure of his hand;

His day's ride is a furlong space,
His city tops a glimmering haze:
I plant his eyes on the sky-hoop bounding; —
See there the grim gray rounding
Of the bullet of the earth
Whereon ye sail,
Tumbling steep
In the uncontinented deep; —
He looks on that, and he turns pale:
'Tis even so, this treacherous kite,
Farm-furrowed, town-incrusted sphere,
Thoughtless of its anxious freight,
Plunges eyeless on for ever,
And he, poor parasite, —
Cooped in a ship he cannot steer,
Who is the captain he knows not,
Port or pilot trows not, —
Risk or ruin he must share.
I scowl on him with my cloud,
With my north wind chill his blood,
I lame him clattering down the rocks,
And to live he is in fear.
Then, at last, I let him down
Once more into his dapper town,

To chatter frightened to his clan,
And forget me, if he can.
As in the old poetic fame
The gods are blind and lame,
And the simular despite
Betrays the more abounding might,
So call not waste that barren cone
Above the floral zone,
Where forests starve:
It is pure use;
What sheaves like those which here we glean
     and bind,
Of a celestial Ceres, and the Muse?

Ages are thy days,
Thou grand expressor of the present tense,
And type of permanence,
Firm ensign of the fatal Being,
Amid these coward shapes of joy and grief
That will not bide the seeing.
Hither we bring
Our insect miseries to the rocks,
And the whole flight with pestering wing
Vanish and end their murmuring,

Vanish beside these dedicated blocks,
Which, who can tell what mason laid?
Spoils of a front none need restore,
Replacing frieze and architrave;
Yet flowers each stone rosette and metope brave,
Still is the haughty pile erect
Of the old building Intellect.
Complement of human kind,
Having us at vantage still,
Our sumptuous indigence,
O barren mound! thy plenties fill.
We fool and prate, —
Thou art silent and sedate.
To million kinds and times one sense
The constant mountain doth dispense,
Shedding on all its snows and leaves, •
One joy it joys, one grief it grieves.
Thou seest, O watchman tall!
Our towns and races grow and fall,
And imagest the stable Good
For which we all our lifetime grope,
In shifting form the formless mind;
And though the substance us elude,
We in thee the shadow find.

Thou in our astronomy
An opaker star,
Seen, haply, from afar,
Above the horizon's hoop.
A moment by the railway troop,
As o'er some bolder height they speed, —
By circumspect ambition,
By errant Gain,
By feasters, and the frivolous, —
Recallest us,
And makest sane.
Mute orator! well-skilled to plead,
And send conviction without phrase,
Thou dost supply
The shortness of our days,
And promise, on thy Founder's truth,
Long morrow to this mortal youth.

FABLE.

THE mountain and the squirrel
Had a quarrel,
And the former called the latter, "little prig":
Bun replied,
You are doubtless very big,
But all sorts of things and weather
Must be taken in together
To make up a year,
And a sphere.
And I think it no disgrace
To occupy my place.
If I'm not so large as you,
You are not so small as I,
And not half so spry:
I'll not deny you make
A very pretty squirrel track;
Talents differ; all is well and wisely put;
If I cannot carry forests on my back,
Neither can you crack a nut.

ODE,

INSCRIBED TO WILLIAM H. CHANNING.

Though loth to grieve
The evil time's sole patriot,
I cannot leave
My buried thought
For the priest's cant,
Or statesman's rant.

If I refuse
My study for their politique,
Which at the best is trick,
The angry muse
Puts confusion in my brain.

But who is he that prates
Of the culture of mankind,
Of better arts and life?
Go, blind worm, go,
Behold the famous States

Harrying Mexico
With rifle and with knife.

Or who, with accent bolder,
Dare praise the freedom-loving mountaineer,
I found by thee, O rushing Contoocook!
And in thy valleys, Agiochook!
The jackals of the negro-holder.

The God who made New Hampshire
Taunted the lofty land
With little men.
Small bat and wren
House in the oak.
If earth fire cleave
The upheaved land, and bury the folk,
The southern crocodile would grieve.

Virtue palters, right is hence,
Freedom praised but hid;
Funeral eloquence
Rattles the coffin-lid.

What boots thy zeal,
O glowing friend,

That would indignant rend
The northland from the south?
Wherefore? To what good end?
Boston Bay and Bunker Hill
Would serve things still:
Things are of the snake.

The horseman serves the horse,
The neat-herd serves the neat,
The merchant serves the purse,
The eater serves his meat;
'Tis the day of the chattel,
Web to weave, and corn to grind,
Things are in the saddle,
And ride mankind.

There are two laws discrete
Not reconciled,
Law for man, and law for thing;
The last builds town and fleet,
But it runs wild,
And doth the man unking.

'Tis fit the forest fall,
The steep be graded,

The mountain tunnelled,
The land shaded,
The orchard planted,
The globe tilled,
The prairie planted,
The steamer built.

Let man serve law for man,
Live for friendship, live for love,
For truth's and harmony's behoof;
The state may follow how it can,
As Olympus follows Jove.
Yet do not I implore
The wrinkled shopman to my sounding woods,
Nor bid the unwilling senator
Ask votes of thrushes in the solitudes.
Every one to his chosen work.
Foolish hands may mix and mar,
Wise and sure the issues are.
Round they roll, till dark is light,
Sex to sex, and even to odd;
The over-God,
Who marries Right to Might,
Who peoples, unpeoples,

He who exterminates
Races by stronger races,
Black by white faces,
Knows to bring honey
Out of the lion,
Grafts gentlest scion
On Pirate and Turk.

The Cossack eats Poland,
Like stolen fruit;
Her last noble is ruined,
Her last poet mute;
Straight into double band
The victors divide,
Half for freedom strike and stand,
The astonished muse finds thousands at her side.

ASTRÆA.

HIMSELF it was who wrote
His rank, and quartered his own coat.
There is no king nor sovereign state
That can fix a hero's rate;
Each to all is venerable,
Cap-a-pie invulnerable,
Until he write, where all eyes rest,
Slave or master on his breast.

I saw men go up and down
In the country and the town,
With this prayer upon their neck,
"Judgment and a judge we seek."
Not to monarchs they repair,
Nor to learned jurist's chair,
But they hurry to their peers,
To their kinsfolk and their dears,
Louder than with speech they pray,
What am I? companion; say.

And the friend not hesitates
To assign just place and mates,
Answers not in word or letter,
Yet is understood the better; —
Is to his friend a looking-glass,
Reflects his figure that doth pass.
Every wayfarer he meets
What himself declared, repeats;
What himself confessed, records;
Sentences him in his words,
The form is his own corporal form,
And his thought the penal worm.

Yet shine for ever virgin minds,
Loved by stars and purest winds,
Which, o'er passion throned sedate,
Have not hazarded their state,
Disconcert the searching spy,
Rendering to a curious eye
The durance of a granite ledge
To those who gaze from the sea's edge.
It is there for benefit,
It is there for purging light,
There for purifying storms,

And its depths reflect all forms;
It cannot parley with the mean,
Pure by impure is not seen.
For there's no sequestered grot,
Lone mountain tarn, or isle forgot,
But justice journeying in the sphere
Daily stoops to harbor there.

ETIENNE DE LA BOÉCE.

I SERVE you not, if you I follow,
Shadow-like, o'er hill and hollow,
And bend my fancy to your leading,
All too nimble for my treading.
When the pilgrimage is done,
And we've the landscape overrun,
I am bitter, vacant, thwarted,
And your heart is unsupported.
Vainly valiant, you have missed
The manhood that should yours resist,
Its complement; but if I could
In severe or cordial mood
Lead you rightly to my altar,
Where the wisest muses falter,
And worship that world-warning spark
Which dazzles me in midnight dark,
Equalizing small and large,
While the soul it doth surcharge,

That the poor is wealthy grown,
And the hermit never alone,
The traveller and the road seem one
With the errand to be done; —
That were a man's and lover's part,
That were Freedom's whitest chart.

"SUUM CUIQUE."

THE rain has spoiled the farmer's day;
Shall sorrow put my books away?
Thereby are two days lost:
Nature shall mind her own affairs,
I will attend my proper cares,
In rain, or sun, or frost.

COMPENSATION.

WHY should I keep holiday,
When other men have none?
Why but because when these are gay,
I sit and mourn alone.

And why when mirth unseals all tongues
Should mine alone be dumb?
Ah! late I spoke to silent throngs,
And now their hour is come.

FORBEARANCE.

Hast thou named all the birds without a gun;
Loved the wood-rose, and left it on its stalk;
At rich men's tables eaten bread and pulse;
Unarmed, faced danger with a heart of trust;
And loved so well a high behavior
In man or maid, that thou from speech re-
    frained,
Nobility more nobly to repay? —
O be my friend, and teach me to be thine!

THE PARK.

THE prosperous and beautiful
To me seem not to wear
The yoke of conscience masterful,
Which galls me everywhere.

I cannot shake off the god;
On my neck he makes his seat;
I look at my face in the glass,
My eyes his eye-balls meet.

Enchanters! enchantresses!
Your gold makes you seem wise:
The morning mist within your grounds
More proudly rolls, more softly lies.

Yet spake yon purple mountain,
Yet said yon ancient wood,
That night or day, that love or crime
Lead all souls to the Good.

THE FORERUNNERS.

Long I followed happy guides, —
I could never reach their sides.
Their step is forth, and, ere the day,
Breaks up their leaguer, and away.
Keen my sense, my heart was young,
Right goodwill my sinews strung,
But no speed of mine avails
To hunt upon their shining trails.
On and away, their hasting feet
Make the morning proud and sweet.
Flowers they strew, I catch the scent,
Or tone of silver instrument
Leaves on the wind melodious trace,
Yet I could never see their face.
On eastern hills I see their smokes
Mixed with mist by distant lochs.
I meet many travellers
Who the road had surely kept, —
They saw not my fine revellers, —

These had crossed them while they slept.
Some had heard their fair report
In the country or the court.
Fleetest couriers alive
Never yet could once arrive,
As they went or they returned,
At the house where these sojourned.
Sometimes their strong speed they slacken,
Though they are not overtaken:
In sleep, their jubilant troop is near,
I tuneful voices overhear,
It may be in wood or waste, —
At unawares 'tis come and passed.
Their near camp my spirit knows
By signs gracious as rainbows.
I thenceforward and long after
Listen for their harp-like laughter,
And carry in my heart for days
Peace that hallows rudest ways. —

"SURSUM CORDA."

Seek not the Spirit, if it hide,
Inexorable to thy zeal:
Baby, do not whine and chide;
Art thou not also real?
Why should'st thou stoop to poor excuse?
Turn on the Accuser roundly; say,
"Here am I, here will I remain
Forever to myself soothfast,
Go thou, sweet Heaven, or, at thy pleasure
    stay." —
Already Heaven with thee its lot has cast,
For it only can absolutely deal.

119

ODE TO BEAUTY.

WHO gave thee, O Beauty!
The keys of this breast,
Too credulous lover
Of blest and unblest?
Say when in lapsed ages
Thee knew I of old;
Or what was the service
For which I was sold?
When first my eyes saw thee,
I found me thy thrall,
By magical drawings,
Sweet tyrant of all!
I drank at thy fountain
False waters of thirst;
Thou intimate stranger,
Thou latest and first!
Thy dangerous glances
Make women of men;
New-born we are melting
Into nature again.

Lavish, lavish promiser,
Nigh persuading gods to err,
Guest of million painted forms
Which in turn thy glory warms,
The frailest leaf, the mossy bark,
The acorn's cup, the raindrop's arc,
The swinging spider's silver line,
The ruby of the drop of wine,
The shining pebble of the pond,
Thou inscribest with a bond
In thy momentary play
Would bankrupt Nature to repay.

Ah! what avails it
To hide or to shun
Whom the Infinite One
Hath granted his throne?
The heaven high over
Is the deep's lover,
The sun and sea
Informed by thee,
Before me run,
And draw me on,
Yet fly me still,

As Fate refuses
To me the heart Fate for me chooses,
Is it that my opulent soul
Was mingled from the generous whole,
Sea valleys and the deep of skies
Furnished several supplies,
And the sands whereof I'm made
Draw me to them self-betrayed?
I turn the proud portfolios
Which hold the grand designs
Of Salvator, of Guercino,
And Piranesi's lines.
I hear the lofty Pæans
Of the masters of the shell,
Who heard the starry music,
And recount the numbers well:
Olympian bards who sung
Divine Ideas below,
Which always find us young,
And always keep us so.
Oft in streets or humblest places
I detect far wandered graces,
Which from Eden wide astray
In lowly homes have lost their way.

Thee gliding through the sea of form,
Like the lightning through the storm,
Somewhat not to be possessed,
Somewhat not to be caressed,
No feet so fleet could ever find,
No perfect form could ever bind.
Thou eternal fugitive
Hovering over all that live,
Quick and skilful to inspire
Sweet extravagant desire,
Starry space and lily bell
Filling with thy roseate smell,
Wilt not give the lips to taste
Of the nectar which thou hast.

All that's good and great with thee
Stands in deep conspiracy.
Thou hast bribed the dark and lonely
To report thy features only,
And the cold and purple morning
Itself with thoughts of thee adorning,
The leafy dell, the city mart,
Equal trophies of thine art,
E'en the flowing azure air

Thou hast touched for my despair,
And if I languish into dreams,
Again I meet the ardent beams.
Queen of things! I dare not die
In Being's deeps past ear and eye,
Lest there I find the same deceiver,
And be the sport of Fate forever.
Dread power, but dear! if God thou be,
Unmake me quite, or give thyself to me.

GIVE ALL TO LOVE.

Give all to love;
Obey thy heart;
Friends, kindred, days,
Estate, good fame,
Plans, credit, and the muse;
Nothing refuse.

'Tis a brave master,
Let it have scope,
Follow it utterly,
Hope beyond hope;
High and more high,
It dives into noon,
With wing unspent,
Untold intent;
But 'tis a god,
Knows its own path,
And the outlets of the sky.

'Tis not for the mean,
It requireth courage stout,
Souls above doubt,
Valor unbending;
Such 'twill reward,
They shall return
More than they were,
And ever ascending.

Leave all for love; —
Yet, hear me, yet,
One word more thy heart behoved,
One pulse more of firm endeavor,
Keep thee to-day,
To-morrow, for ever,
Free as an Arab
Of thy beloved.
Cling with life to the maid;
But when the surprise,
Vague shadow of surmise,
Flits across her bosom young
Of a joy apart from thee,
Free be she, fancy-free,
Do not thou detain a hem,

Nor the palest rose she flung
From her summer diadem.

Though thou loved her as thyself,
As a self of purer clay,
Tho' her parting dims the day,
Stealing grace from all alive,
Heartily know,
When half-gods go,
The gods arrive.

TO ELLEN, AT THE SOUTH.

THE green grass is growing,
The morning wind is in it,
'Tis a tune worth the knowing,
Though it change every minute.

'Tis a tune of the spring,
Every year plays it over,
To the robin on the wing,
To the pausing lover.

O'er ten thousand thousand acres
Goes light the nimble zephyr,
The flowers, tiny feet of shakers,
Worship him ever.

Hark to the winning sound!
They summon thee, dearest,
Saying; "We have drest for thee the ground,
Nor yet thou appearest.

"O hasten, 'tis our time,
Ere yet the red summer
Scorch our delicate prime,
Loved of bee, the tawny hummer.

"O pride of thy race!
Sad in sooth it were to ours,
If our brief tribe miss thy face, —
We pour New England flowers.

"Fairest! choose the fairest members
Of our lithe society;
June's glories and September's
Show our love and piety.

"Thou shalt command us all,
April's cowslip, summer's clover,
To the gentian in the fall,
Blue-eyed pet of blue-eyed lover.

"O come, then, quickly come,
We are budding, we are blowing,
And the wind which we perfume
Sings a tune that's worth thy knowing."

TO EVA.

O FAIR and stately maid, whose eye
Was kindled in the upper sky
At the same torch that lighted mine;
For so I must interpret still
Thy sweet dominion o'er my will,
A sympathy divine.

Ah! let me blameless gaze upon
Features that seem in heart my own,
Nor fear those watchful sentinels
Which charm the more their glance forbids,
Chaste glowing underneath their lids
With fire that draws while it repels.

—◆—

THINE eyes still shined for me, though far
I lonely roved the land or sea,
As I behold yon evening star,
Which yet beholds not me.

This morn I climbed the misty hill,
And roamed the pastures through;
How danced thy form before my path,
Amidst the deep-eyed dew!

When the red bird spread his sable wing,
And showed his side of flame,
When the rose-bud ripened to the rose,
In both I read thy name.

THE AMULET.

Your picture smiles as first it smiled,
The ring you gave is still the same,
Your letter tells, O changing child,
No tidings *since* it came.

Give me an amulet
That keeps intelligence with you,
Red when you love, and rosier red,
And when you love not, pale and blue.

Alas, that neither bonds nor vows
Can certify possession;
Torments me still the fear that love
Died in its last expression.

132

EROS.

THE sense of the world is short,
Long and various the report, —
To love and be beloved;
Men and gods have not outlearned it,
And how oft soe'er they've turned it,
'Tis not to be improved.

133

HERMIONE.

ON a mound an Arab lay,
And sung his sweet regrets,
And told his amulets;
The summer bird
His sorrow heard,
And when he heaved a sigh profound
The sympathetic swallows swept the ground.

If it be as they said, she was not fair;
Beauty's not beautiful to me,
But sceptred Genius aye inorbed,
Culminating in her sphere.
This Hermione absorbed
The lustre of the land and ocean,
Hills and islands, vine and tree,
In her form and motion.
I ask no bauble miniature,
Nor ringlets dead
Shorn from her comely head,

Now that morning not disdains, —
Mountains and the misty plains —
Her colossal portraiture:
They her heralds be,
Steeped in her quality,
And singers of her fame,
Who is their muse and dame.

Higher, dear swallows, mind not what I say.
Ah! heedless how the weak are strong,
Say, was it just
In thee to frame, in me to trust,
Thou to the Syrian couldst belong?

I am of a lineage
That each for each doth fast engage.
In old Bassora's schools I seemed
Hermit vowed to books and gloom,
Ill-bested for gay bridegroom:
I was by thy touch redeemed;
When thy meteor glances came,
We talked at large of worldly Fate,
And drew truly every trait.
Once I dwelt apart,

Now I live with all;
As shepherd's lamp on far hill side,
Seems, by the traveller espied,
A door into the mountain heart,
So didst thou quarry and unlock
Highways for me through the rock.

Now deceived thou wanderest
In strange lands, unblest,
And my kindred come to soothe me,
South wind is my next of blood;
He is come through fragrant wood,
Drugged with spice from climates warm,
And in every twinkling glade,
And twilight nook,
Unveils thy form:
Out of the forest way
Forth paced it yesterday,
And, when I sat by the water-course,
Watching the daylight fade,
It throbbed up from the brook.
River, and rose, and crag, and bird,
Frost, and sun, and eldest night
To me their aid preferred,

To me their comfort plight:
"Courage! we are thine allies;
And with this hint be wise,
The chains of kind
The distant bind:
Deed thou doest, she must do,
Above her will, be true;
And, in her strict resort
To winds and waterfalls,
And autumn's sun-lit festivals,
To music, and to music's thought,
Inextricably bound,
She shall find thee, and be found.
Follow not her flying feet,
Come to us herself to meet."

ODE.

I.

INITIAL LOVE.

VENUS, when her son was lost,
Cried him up and down the coast,
In hamlets, palaces, and parks,
And told the truant by his marks,
Golden curls, and quiver, and bow; —
This befell long ago.
Time and tide are strangely changed,
Men and manners much deranged;
None will now find Cupid latent
By this foolish antique patent.
He came late along the waste,
Shod like a traveller for haste,
With malice dared me to proclaim him,
That the maids and boys might name him.

Boy no more, he wears all coats,
Frocks, and blouses, capes, capôtes,

He bears no bow, or quiver, or wand,
Nor chaplet on his head or hand:
Leave his weeds and heed his eyes,
All the rest he can disguise.
In the pit of his eyes a spark
Would bring back day if it were dark,
And, — if I tell you all my thought,
Though I comprehend it not, —
In those unfathomable orbs
Every function he absorbs;
He doth eat, and drink, and fish, and shoot,
And write, and reason, and compute,
And ride, and run, and have, and hold,
And whine, and flatter, and regret,
And kiss, and couple, and beget,
By those roving eye-balls bold;
Undaunted are their courages,
Right Cossacks in their forages;
Fleeter they than any creature,
They are his steeds and not his feature,
Inquisitive, and fierce, and fasting,
Restless, predatory, hasting, —
And they pounce on other eyes,
As lions on their prey;

And round their circles is writ,
Plainer than the day,
Underneath, within, above,
Love, love, love, love.
He lives in his eyes,
There doth digest, and work, and spin,
And buy, and sell, and lose, and win;
He rolls them with delighted motion,
Joy-tides swell their mimic ocean.
Yet holds he them with tortest rein,
That they may seize and entertain
The glance that to their glance opposes,
Like fiery honey sucked from roses.

He palmistry can understand,
Imbibing virtue by his hand
As if it were a living root;
The pulse of hands will make him mute;
With all his force he gathers balms
Into those wise thrilling palms.

Cupid is a casuist,
A mystic, and a cabalist,
Can your lurking Thought surprise,

And interpret your device;
Mainly versed in occult science,
In magic, and in clairvoyance.
Oft he keeps his fine ear strained,
And reason on her tiptoe pained,
For aery intelligence,
And for strange coincidence.
But it touches his quick heart
When Fate by omens takes his part,
And chance-dropt hints from Nature's sphere
Deeply soothe his anxious ear.

Heralds high before him run,
He has ushers many a one,
Spreads his welcome where he goes,
And touches all things with his rose.
All things wait for and divine him, —
How shall I dare to malign him,
Or accuse the god of sport? —
I must end my true report,
Painting him from head to foot,
In as far as I took note,
Trusting well the matchless power
Of this young-eyed emperor

Will clear his fame from every cloud,
With the bards, and with the crowd.

He is wilful, mutable,
Shy, untamed, inscrutable,
Swifter-fashioned than the fairies,
Substance mixed of pure contraries,
His vice some elder virtue's token,
And his good is evil spoken.
Failing sometimes of his own,
He is headstrong and alone;
He affects the wood and wild,
Like a flower-hunting child,
Buries himself in summer waves,
In trees, with beasts, in mines, and caves,
Loves nature like a horned cow,
Bird, or deer, or cariboo.

Shun him, nymphs, on the fleet horses!
He has a total world of wit,
O how wise are his discourses!
But he is the arch-hypocrite,
And through all science and all art,
Seeks alone his counterpart.
He is a Pundit of the east,

He is an augur and a priest,
And his soul will melt in prayer,
But word and wisdom are a snare;
Corrupted by the present toy,
He follows joy, and only joy.

There is no mask but he will wear,
He invented oaths to swear,
He paints, he carves, he chants, he prays,
And holds all stars in his embrace,
Godlike, — but 'tis for his fine pelf,
The social quintessence of self.
Well, said I, he is hypocrite,
And folly the end of his subtle wit,
He takes a sovran privilege
Not allowed to any liege,
For he does go behind all law,
And right into himself does draw,
For he is sovranly allied.
Heaven's oldest blood flows in his side,
And interchangeably at one
With every king on every throne,
That no God dare say him nay,
Or see the fault, or seen betray;

He has the Muses by the heart,
And the Parcæ all are of his part.

His many signs cannot be told,
He has not one mode, but manifold,
Many fashions and addresses,
Piques, reproaches, hurts, caresses,
Action, service, badinage,
He will preach like a friar,
And jump like Harlequin,
He will read like a crier,
And fight like a Paladin.
Boundless is his memory,
Plans immense his term prolong,
He is not of counted age,
Meaning always to be young.
And his wish is intimacy,
Intimater intimacy,
And a stricter privacy,
The impossible shall yet be done,
And being two shall still be one.
As the wave breaks to foam on shelves,
Then runs into a wave again,
So lovers melt their sundered selves,
Yet melted would be twain.

II.

THE DÆMONIC AND THE CELESTIAL LOVE.

DÆMONIC LOVE.

MAN was made of social earth,
Child and brother from his birth;
Tethered by a liquid cord
Of blood through veins of kindred poured,
Next his heart the fireside band
Of mother, father, sister, stand;
Names from awful childhood heard,
Throbs of a wild religion stirred,
Their good was heaven, their harm was vice,
Till Beauty came to snap all ties,
The maid, abolishing the past,
With lotus-wine obliterates
Dear memory's stone-incarved traits,
And by herself supplants alone
Friends year by year more inly known.

When her calm eyes opened bright,
All were foreign in their light.
It was ever the self-same tale,
The old experience will not fail, —
Only two in the garden walked,
And with snake and seraph talked.

But God said;
I will have a purer gift,
There is smoke in the flame;
New flowerets bring, new prayers uplift,
And love without a name.
Fond children, ye desire
To please each other well;
Another round, a higher,
Ye shall climb on the heavenly stair,
And selfish preference forbear;
And in right deserving,
And without a swerving
Each from your proper state,
Weave roses for your mate.

Deep, deep are loving eyes,
Flowed with naphtha fiery sweet,

And the point is Paradise
Where their glances meet:
Their reach shall yet be more profound,
And a vision without bound:
The axis of those eyes sun-clear
Be the axis of the sphere;
Then shall the lights ye pour amain
Go without check or intervals,
Through from the empyrean walls,
Unto the same again.

Close, close to men,
Like undulating layer of air,
Right above their heads,
The potent plain of Dæmons spreads.
Stands to each human soul its own,
For watch, and ward, and furtherance
In the snares of nature's dance;
And the lustre and the grace
Which fascinate each human heart,
Beaming from another part,
Translucent through the mortal covers,
Is the Dæmon's form and face.
To and fro the Genius hies,

A gleam which plays and hovers
Over the maiden's head,
And dips sometimes as low as to her eyes.

Unknown, — albeit lying near, —
To men the path to the Dæmon sphere,
And they that swiftly come and go,
Leave no track on the heavenly snow.
Sometimes the airy synod bends,
And the mighty choir descends,
And the brains of men thenceforth,
In crowded and in still resorts,
Teem with unwonted thoughts.
As when a shower of meteors
Cross the orbit of the earth,
And, lit by fringent air,
Blaze near and far.
Mortals deem the planets bright
Have slipped their sacred bars,
And the lone seaman all the night
Sails astonished amid stars.

Beauty of a richer vein,
Graces of a subtler strain,

Unto men these moon-men lend,
And our shrinking sky extend.
So is man's narrow path
By strength and terror skirted,
Also (from the song the wrath
Of the Genii be averted!
The Muse the truth uncolored speaking),
The Dæmons are self-seeking;
Their fierce and limitary will
Draws men to their likeness still.

The erring painter made Love blind,
Highest Love who shines on all;
Him radiant, sharpest-sighted god
None can bewilder;
Whose eyes pierce
The Universe,
Path-finder, road-builder,
Mediator, royal giver,
Rightly-seeing, rightly-seen,
Of joyful and transparent mien.
'Tis a sparkle passing
From each to each, from me to thee,
Perpetually,

Sharing all, daring all,
Levelling, misplacing
Each obstruction, it unites
Equals remote, and seeming opposites.
And ever and forever Love
Delights to build a road;
Unheeded Danger near him strides,
Love laughs, and on a lion rides.
But Cupid wears another face
Born into Dæmons less divine,
His roses bleach apace,
His nectar smacks of wine.
The Dæmon ever builds a wall,
Himself incloses and includes,
Solitude in solitudes:
In like sort his love doth fall.
He is an oligarch,
He prizes wonder, fame, and mark,
He loveth crowns,
He scorneth drones;
He doth elect
The beautiful and fortunate,
And the sons of intellect,
And the souls of ample fate,

Who the Future's gates unbar,
Minions of the Morning Star.
In his prowess he exults,
And the multitude insults.
His impatient looks devour
Oft the humble and the poor,
And, seeing his eye glare,
They drop their few pale flowers
Gathered with hope to please
Along the mountain towers,
Lose courage, and despair.
He will never be gainsaid,
Pitiless, will not be stayed.
His hot tyranny
Burns up every other tie;
Therefore comes an hour from Jove
Which his ruthless will defies,
And the dogs of Fate unties.
Shiver the palaces of glass,
Shrivel the rainbow-colored walls
Where in bright art each god and sibyl dwelt
Secure as in the Zodiack's belt;
And the galleries and halls
Wherein every Siren sung,

Like a meteor pass.
For this fortune wanted root
In the core of God's abysm,
Was a weed of self and schism:
And ever the Dæmonic Love
Is the ancestor of wars,
And the parent of remorse.

CELESTIAL LOVE.

HIGHER far,
Upward, into the pure realm,
Over sun or star,
Over the flickering Dæmon film,
Thou must mount for love, —
Into vision which all form
In one only form dissolves;
In a region where the wheel,
On which all beings ride,
Visibly revolves;
Where the starred eternal worm
Girds the world with bound and term;
Where unlike things are like,
When good and ill,

And joy and moan,
Melt into one.
There Past, Present, Future, shoot
Triple blossoms from one root
Substances at base divided
In their summits are united,
There the holy Essence rolls,
One through separated souls,
And the sunny Æon sleeps
Folding nature in its deeps,
And every fair and every good
Known in part or known impure
To men below,
In their archetypes endure.

The race of gods,
Or those we erring own,
Are shadows flitting up and down
In the still abodes.
The circles of that sea are laws,
Which publish and which hide the Cause.
Pray for a beam
Out of that sphere
Thee to guide and to redeem.

O what a load
Of care and toil
By lying Use bestowed,
From his shoulders falls, who sees
The true astronomy,
The period of peace!
Counsel which the ages kept,
Shall the well-born soul accept.
As the overhanging trees
Fill the lake with images,
As garment draws the garment's hem
Men their fortunes bring with them;
By right or wrong,
Lands and goods go to the strong;
Property will brutely draw
Still to the proprietor,
Silver to silver creep and wind,
And kind to kind,
Nor less the eternal poles
Of tendency distribute souls.
There need no vows to bind
Whom not each other seek but find.
They give and take no pledge or oath,
Nature is the bond of both.

No prayer persuades, no flattery fawns,
Their noble meanings are their pawns.
Plain and cold is their address,
Power have they for tenderness,
And so thoroughly is known
Each others' purpose by his own,
They can parley without meeting,
Need is none of forms of greeting,
They can well communicate
In their innermost estate;
When each the other shall avoid,
Shall each by each be most enjoyed.
Not with scarfs or perfumed gloves
Do these celebrate their loves,
Not by jewels, feasts, and savors,
Not by ribbons or by favors,
But by the sun-spark on the sea,
And the cloud-shadow on the lea,
The soothing lapse of morn to mirk,
And the cheerful round of work.
Their cords of love so public are,
They intertwine the farthest star.
The throbbing sea, the quaking earth,
Yield sympathy and signs of mirth;

Is none so high, so mean is none,
But feels and seals this union.
Even the fell Furies are appeased,
The good applaud, the lost are eased.

Love's hearts are faithful, but not fond,
Bound for the just, but not beyond;
Not glad, as the low-loving herd,
Of self in others still preferred,
But they have heartily designed
The benefit of broad mankind.
And they serve men austerely,
After their own genius, clearly,
Without a false humility;
For this is love's nobility,
Not to scatter bread and gold,
Goods and raiment bought and sold, .
But to hold fast his simple sense,
And speak the speech of innocence,
And with hand, and body, and blood,
To make his bosom-counsel good:
For he that feeds men, serveth few,
He serves all, who dares be true.

THE APOLOGY.

THINK me not unkind and rude,
That I walk alone in grove and glen;
I go to the god of the wood
To fetch his word to men.

Tax not my sloth that I
Fold my arms beside the brook;
Each cloud that floated in the sky
Writes a letter in my book.

Chide me not, laborious band,
For the idle flowers I brought;
Every aster in my hand
Goes home loaded with a thought.

There was never mystery,
But 'tis figured in the flowers,
Was never secret history,
But birds tell it in the bowers.

One harvest from thy field
Homeward brought the oxen strong;
A second crop thine acres yield,
Which I gather in a song.

MERLIN.

I.

THY trivial harp will never please
Or fill my craving ear;
Its chords should ring as blows the breeze,
Free, peremptory, clear.
No jingling serenader's art,
Nor tinkle of piano strings,
Can make the wild blood start
In its mystic springs.
The kingly bard
Must smite the chords rudely and hard,
As with hammer or with mace,
That they may render back
Artful thunder that conveys
Secrets of the solar track,
Sparks of the supersolar blaze.
Merlin's blows are strokes of fate,
Chiming with the forest-tone,
When boughs buffet boughs in the wood;

Chiming with the gasp and moan
Of the ice-imprisoned flood;
With the pulse of manly hearts,
With the voice of orators,
With the din of city arts,
With the cannonade of wars.
With the marches of the brave,
And prayers of might from martyrs' cave.

Great is the art,
Great be the manners of the bard!
He shall not his brain encumber
With the coil of rhythm and number,
But, leaving rule and pale forethought,
He shall aye climb
For his rhyme:
Pass in, pass in, the angels say,
In to the upper doors;
Nor count compartments of the floors,
But mount to Paradise
By the stairway of surprise.

Blameless master of the games,
King of sport that never shames;

He shall daily joy dispense
Hid in song's sweet influence.
Things more cheerly live and go,
What time the subtle mind
Plays aloud the tune whereto
Their pulses beat,
And march their feet,
And their members are combined.

By Sybarites beguiled
He shall no task decline;
Merlin's mighty line,
Extremes of nature reconciled,
Bereaved a tyrant of his will,
And made the lion mild.
Songs can the tempest still,
Scattered on the stormy air,
Mould the year to fair increase,
And bring in poetic peace.

He shall not seek to weave,
In weak unhappy times,
Efficacious rhymes;
Wait his returning strength,

Bird, that from the nadir's floor,
To the zenith's top could soar,
The soaring orbit of the muse exceeds that
    journey's length!

Nor, profane, affect to hit
Or compass that by meddling wit,
Which only the propitious mind
Publishes when 'tis inclined.
There are open hours
When the god's will sallies free,
And the dull idiot might see
The flowing fortunes of a thousand years;
Sudden, at unawares,
Self-moved fly-to the doors,
Nor sword of angels could reveal
What they conceal.

MERLIN.

II.

THE rhyme of the poet
Modulates the king's affairs,
Balance-loving nature
Made all things in pairs.
To every foot its antipode,
Each color with its counter glowed,
To every tone beat answering tones,
Higher or graver;
Flavor gladly blends with flavor;
Leaf answers leaf upon the bough,
And match the paired cotyledons.
Hands to hands, and feet to feet,
In one body grooms and brides;
Eldest rite, two married sides
In every mortal meet.
Light's far furnace shines,
Smelting balls and bars,
Forging double stars,

Glittering twins and trines.
The animals are sick with love,
Lovesick with rhyme;
Each with all propitious Time
Into chorus wove.

Like the dancers' ordered band,
Thoughts come also hand in hand,
In equal couples mated,
Or else alternated,
Adding by their mutual gage
One to other health and age.
Solitary fancies go
Short-lived wandering to and fro,
Most like to bachelors,
Or an ungiven maid,
Not ancestors,
With no posterity to make the lie afraid,
Or keep truth undecayed.

Perfect paired as eagle's wings,
Justice is the rhyme of things;
Trade and counting use
The self-same tuneful muse;

And Nemesis,
Who with even matches odd,
Who athwart space redresses
The partial wrong,
Fills the just period,
And finishes the song.

Subtle rhymes with ruin rife
Murmur in the house of life,
Sung by the Sisters as they spin;
In perfect time and measure, they
Build and unbuild our echoing clay,
As the two twilights of the day
Fold us music-drunken in.

BACCHUS.

Bring me wine, but wine which never grew
In the belly of the grape,
Or grew on vine whose taproots reaching through
Under the Andes to the Cape,
Suffered no savor of the world to 'scape.
Let its grapes the morn salute
From a nocturnal root
Which feels the acrid juice
Of Styx and Erebus,
And turns the woe of night,
By its own craft, to a more rich delight.

We buy ashes for bread,
We buy diluted wine;
Give me of the true,
Whose ample leaves and tendrils curled
Among the silver hills of heaven,
Draw everlasting dew;
Wine of wine,

Blood of the world,
Form of forms and mould of statures,
That I, intoxicated,
And by the draught assimilated,
May float at pleasure through all natures,
The bird-language rightly spell,
And that which roses say so well.

Wine that is shed
Like the torrents of the sun
Up the horizon walls;
Or like the Atlantic streams which run
When the South Sea calls.

Water and bread;
Food which needs no transmuting,
Rainbow-flowering, wisdom-fruiting;
Wine which is already man,
Food which teach and reason can.

Wine which music is;
Music and wine are one;
That I, drinking this,
Shall hear far chaos talk with me,

Kings unborn shall walk with me,
And the poor grass shall plot and plan
What it will do when it is man:
Quickened so, will I unlock
Every crypt of every rock.

I thank the joyful juice
For all I know;
Winds of remembering
Of the ancient being blow,
And seeming-solid walls of use
Open and flow.

Pour, Bacchus, the remembering wine;
Retrieve the loss of me and mine;
Vine for vine be antidote,
And the grape requite the lote.
Haste to cure the old despair,
Reason in nature's lotus drenched,
The memory of ages quenched; —
Give them again to shine.
Let wine repair what this undid,
And where the infection slid,
And dazzling memory revive.

Refresh the faded tints,
Recut the aged prints,
And write my old adventures, with the pen
Which, on the first day, drew
Upon the tablets blue
The dancing Pleiads, and the eternal men.

LOSS AND GAIN.

Virtue runs before the muse
And defies her skill,
She is rapt, and doth refuse
To wait a painter's will.

Star-adoring, occupied,
Virtue cannot bend her,
Just to please a poet's pride,
To parade her splendor.

The bard must be with good intent
No more his, but hers,
Throw away his pen and paint,
Kneel with worshippers.

Then, perchance, a sunny ray
From the heaven of fire,
His lost tools may over-pay,
And better his desire.

MEROPS.

WHAT care I, so they stand the same, —
Things of the heavenly mind, —
How long the power to give them fame
Tarries yet behind?

Thus far to-day your favors reach,
O fair, appeasing Presences!
Ye taught my lips a single speech,
And a thousand silences.

Space grants beyond his fated road
No inch to the god of day,
And copious language still bestowed
One word, no more, to say.

THE HOUSE.

THERE is no architect
Can build as the muse can;
She is skilful to select
Materials for her plan;

Slow and warily to choose
Rafters of immortal pine,
Or cedar incorruptible,
Worthy her design.

She threads dark Alpine forests,
Or valleys by the sea,
In many lands, with painful steps,
Ere she can find a tree.

She ransacks mines and ledges,
And quarries every rock,
To hew the famous adamant,
For each eternal block.

She lays her beams in music,
In music every one,
To the cadence of the whirling world
Which dances round the sun.

That so they shall not be displaced
By lapses or by wars,
But for the love of happy souls
Outlive the newest stars.

SAADI.

TREES in groves,
Kine in droves,
In ocean sport the scaly herds,
Wedge-like cleave the air the birds,
To northern lakes fly wind-borne ducks,
Browse the mountain sheep in flocks,
Men consort in camp and town,
But the poet dwells alone.

God who gave to him the lyre,
Of all mortals the desire,
For all breathing men's behoof,
Straitly charged him, "Sit aloof;"
Annexed a warning, poets say,
To the bright premium, —
Ever when twain together play,
Shall the harp be dumb.
Many may come,
But one shall sing;

Two touch the string,
The harp is dumb.
Though there come a million
Wise Saadi dwells alone.

Yet Saadi loved the race of men, —
No churl immured in cave or den, —
In bower and hall
He wants them all,
Nor can dispense
With Persia for his audience;
They must give ear,
Grow red with joy, and white with fear,
Yet he has no companion,
Come ten, or come a million,
Good Saadi dwells alone.

Be thou ware where Saadi dwells.
Gladly round that golden lamp
Sylvan deities encamp,
And simple maids and noble youth
Are welcome to the man of truth.
Most welcome they who need him most,
They feed the spring which they exhaust:

For greater need
Draws better deed:
But, critic, spare thy vanity,
Nor show thy pompous parts,
To vex with odious subtlety
The cheerer of men's hearts.

Sad-eyed Fakirs swiftly say
Endless dirges to decay;
Never in the blaze of .light
Lose the shudder of midnight;
And at overflowing noon,
Hear wolves barking at the moon;
In the bower of dalliance sweet
Hear the far Avenger's feet;
And shake before those awful Powers
Who in their pride forgive not ours.
Thus the sad-eyed Fakirs preach;
"Bard, when thee would Allah teach,
And lift thee to his holy mount,
He sends thee from his bitter fount,
Wormwood; saying, Go thy ways,
Drink not the Malaga of praise,
But do the deed thy fellows hate,

And compromise thy peaceful state.
Smite the white breasts which thee fed,
Stuff sharp thorns beneath the head
Of them thou shouldst have comforted.
For out of woe and out of crime
Draws the heart a lore sublime."
And yet it seemeth not to me
That the high gods love tragedy;
For Saadi sat in the sun,
And thanks was his contrition;
For haircloth and for bloody whips,
Had active hands and smiling lips;
And yet his runes he rightly read,
And to his folk his message sped.
Sunshine in his heart transferred
Lighted each transparent word;
And well could honoring Persia learn
What Saadi wished to say;
For Saadi's nightly stars did burn
Brighter than Dschami's day.

Whispered the muse in Saadi's cot;
O gentle Saadi, listen not,
Tempted by thy praise of wit,

Or by thirst and appetite
For the talents not thine own,
To sons of contradiction.
Never, sun of eastern morning,
Follow falsehood, follow scorning,
Denounce who will, who will, deny,
And pile the hills to scale the sky;
Let theist, atheist, pantheist,
Define and wrangle how they list, —
Fierce conserver, fierce destroyer,
But thou joy-giver and enjoyer,
Unknowing war, unknowing crime,
Gentle Saadi, mind thy rhyme.
Heed not what the brawlers say,
Heed thou only Saadi's lay.

Let the great world bustle on
With war and trade, with camp and town.
A thousand men shall dig and eat,
At forge and furnace thousands sweat,
And thousands sail the purple sea,
And give or take the stroke of war,
Or crowd the market and bazaar.
Oft shall war end, and peace return,

And cities rise where cities burn,
Ere one man my hill shall climb,
Who can turn the golden rhyme;
Let them manage how they may,
Heed thou only Saadi's lay.
Seek the living among the dead:
Man in man is imprisoned.
Barefooted Dervish is not poor,
If fate unlock his bosom's door.
So that what his eye hath seen
His tongue can paint, as bright, as keen,
And what his tender heart hath felt,
With equal fire thy heart shall melt.
For, whom the muses shine upon,
And touch with soft persuasion,
His words like a storm-wind can bring
Terror and beauty on their wing;
In his every syllable
Lurketh nature veritable;
And though he speak in midnight dark,
In heaven, no star; on earth, no spark;
Yet before the listener's eye
Swims the world in ecstasy,
The forest waves, the morning breaks,

The pastures sleep, ripple the lakes,
Leaves twinkle, flowers like persons be,
And life pulsates in rock or tree.
Saadi! so far thy words shall reach;
Suns rise and set in Saadi's speech.

And thus to Saadi said the muse;
Eat thou the bread which men refuse;
Flee from the goods which from thee flee;
Seek nothing; Fortune seeketh thee.
Nor mount, nor dive; all good things keep
The midway of the eternal deep;
Wish not to fill the isles with eyes
To fetch thee birds of paradise;
On thine orchard's edge belong
All the brass of plume and song;
Wise Ali's sunbright sayings pass
For proverbs in the market-place;
Through mountains bored by regal art
Toil whistles as he drives his cart.
Nor scour the seas, nor sift mankind,
A poet or a friend to find;
Behold, he watches at the door,
Behold his shadow on the floor.

Open innumerable doors,
The heaven where unveiled Allah pours
The flood of truth, the flood of good,
The seraph's and the cherub's food;
Those doors are men; the pariah kind
Admits thee to the perfect Mind.
Seek not beyond thy cottage wall
Redeemer that can yield thee all.
While thou sittest at thy door,
On the desert's yellow floor,
Listening to the gray-haired crones,
Foolish gossips, ancient drones, —
Saadi, see, they rise in stature
To the height of mighty nature,
And the secret stands revealed
Fraudulent Time in vain concealed,
That blessed gods in servile masks
Plied for thee thy household tasks.

HOLIDAYS.

From fall to spring the russet acorn,
Fruit beloved of maid and boy,
Lent itself beneath the forest
To be the children's toy.

Pluck it now; in vain: thou canst not,
Its root has pierced yon shady mound,
Toy no longer, it has duties;
It is anchored in the ground.

Year by year the rose-lipped maiden,
Play-fellow of young and old,
Was frolic sunshine, dear to all men,
More dear to one than mines of gold.

Whither went the lovely hoyden?—
Disappeared in blessed wife,
Servant to a wooden cradle,
Living in a baby's life.

Still thou playest; — short vacation
Fate grants each to stand aside;
Now must thou be man and artist;
'Tis the turning of the tide.

PAINTING AND SCULPTURE.

THE sinful painter drapes his goddess warm,
Because she still is naked, being drest;
The godlike sculptor will not so deform
Beauty, which bones and flesh enough invest.

184

FROM THE PERSIAN OF HAFIZ.

[The Poems of Hafiz are held by the Persians to be mystical and allegorical. The following ode, notwithstanding its anacreontic style, is regarded by his German editor, Von Hammer, as one of those which earned for Hafiz among his countrymen the title of "Tongue of the Secret."]

BUTLER, fetch the ruby wine,
Which with sudden greatness fills us;
Pour for me who in my spirit
Fail in courage and performance;
Bring the philosophic stone,
Karun's treasure, Noah's life;
Haste, that by thy means I open
All the doors of luck and life.
Bring me, boy, the fire-water
Zoroaster sought in dust.
To Hafiz revelling 'tis allowed
To pray to Matter and to Fire.
Bring the wine of Jamschid's glass
That shone, ere time was, in the Néant.

Give it me, that through its virtue
I, as Jamschid, see through worlds.
Wisely said the Kaiser Jamschid,
This world's not worth a barleycorn.
Bring me, boy, the nectar cup,
Since it leads to Paradise.
Flute and lyre lordly speak,
Lees of wine outvalue crowns.
Hither bring the veiled beauty
Who in ill-famed houses sits:
Lead her forth: my honest name
Freely barter I for wine.
Bring me, boy, the fire-water,
Drinks the lion — the woods burn.
Give it me, that I storm heaven,
Tear the net from the arch-wolf.
Wine, wherewith the Houris teach
Angels the ways of Paradise.
On the glowing coals I'll set it,
And therewith my brain perfume.
Bring me wine, through whose effulgence
Jam and Chosroes yielded light:
Wine, that to the flute I sing
Where is Jam, and where is Kauss.

Bring the blessing of old times;
Bless the old departed Shahs;
Bring it me, the Shah of hearts.
Bring me wine to wash me clean,
Of the weather-stains of care,
See the countenance of luck.
While I dwell in spirit-gardens,
Wherefore sit I shackled here?
Lo, this mirror shows me all.
Drunk, I speak of purity,
Beggar, I of lordship speak.
When Hafiz in his revel sings,
Shouteth Sohra in her sphere.

Fear the changes of a day:
Bring wine which increases life,
Since the world is all untrue,
Let the trumpets thee remind
How the crown of Kobad vanished.
Be not certain of the world;
'Twill not spare to shed thy blood.
Desperate of the world's affair,
Came I running to the wine-house.
Give me wine which maketh glad,

That I may my steed bestride,
Through the course career with Rustem,
Gallop to my heart's content.
Give me, boy, the ruby cup
Which unlocks the heart with wine,
That I reason quite renounce,
And plant banners on the worlds.
Let us make our glasses kiss,
Let us quench the sorrow-cinders:
To-day let us drink together.
Whoso has a banquet dressed,
Is with glad mind satisfied,
'Scaping from the snares of Dews.

Alas for youth! 'tis gone in wind, —
Happy he who spent it well.
Give me wine, that I o'erleap
Both worlds at a single spring,
Stole at dawn from glowing spheres
Call of Houris to mine ear;
"O happy bird! delicious soul!
Spread thy pinion, break the cage;
Sit on the roof of the seven domes,
Where the spirit takes repose."
In the time of Bisurdschimihr,

Menutscheher's beauty shined,
On the beaker of Nushirvan,
Wrote they once in elder times,
"Hear the Counsel, learn from us
Sample of the course of things;
Earth, it is a place of sorrow,
Scanty joys are here below,
Who has nothing, has no sorrow."

Where is Jam, and where his cup?
Solomon, and his mirror where?
Which of the wise masters knows
What time Kauss and Jam existed?
When those heroes left this world,
Left they nothing but their names.
Bind thy heart not to the earth,
When thou goest, come not back.
Fools squander on the world their hearts.
League with it, is feud with heaven;
Never gives it what thou wishest.

A cup of wine imparts the sight
Of the five heaven-domes with nine steps:
Whoso can himself renounce,
Without support shall walk thereon.

Who discreet is, is not wise.
Give me, boy, the Kaiser cup,
Which rejoices heart and soul;   '
Under type of wine and cup
Signify we purest love.
Youth like lightning disappears,
Life goes by us as the wind:
Leave the dwelling with six doors,
And the serpent with nine heads;
Life and silver spend thou freely,
If thou honorest the soul.
Haste into the other life;
All is nought save God alone.   ·
Give me, boy, this toy of dæmons.
When the cup of Jam was lost,
Him availed the world no more.
Fetch the wine-glass made of ice,
Wake the torpid heart with wine.
Every clod of loam below us
Is a skull of Alexander;
Oceans are the blood of princes;
Desert sands the dust of beauties.
More than one Darius was there
Who the whole world overcame;

But since these gave up the ghost,
Thinkest thou they never were?
Boy, go from me to the Shah,
Say to him : Shah crowned as Jam,
Win thou first the poor man's heart,
Then the glass; so know the world.
Empty sorrows from the earth
Canst thou drive away with wine.
Now in thy throne's recent beauty,
In the flowing tide of power,
Moon of fortune, mighty king,
Whose tiara sheddeth lustre,
Peace secure to fish and fowl,
Heart and eye-sparkle to saints;
Shoreless is the sea of praise, —
I content me with a prayer.
From Nisami's poet-works,
Highest ornament of speech,
Here a verse will I recite,
Verse as beautiful as pearls.
"More kingdoms wait thy diadem,
Than are known to thee by name;
May the sovran destiny
Grant a victory every morn!"

FROM THE PERSIAN OF HAFIZ.

Of Paradise, O hermit wise,
Let us renounce the thought.
Of old therein our names of sin
Allah recorded not.

Who dear to God on earthly sod
No corn-grain plants,
The same is glad that life is had,
Though corn he wants.

Thy mind the mosque and cool kiosk,
Spare fast, and orisons;
Mine me allows the drink-house,
And sweet chase of the nuns.

O just fakeer, with brow austere,
Forbid me not the vine;
On the first day, poor Hafiz clay
Was kneaded up with wine.

He is no dervise, Heaven slights his service,
Who shall refuse
There in the banquet, to pawn his blanket
For Schiraz's juice.

Who his friend's shirt, or hem of his shirt,
Shall spare to pledge,
To him Eden's bliss and Angel's kiss
Shall want their edge.

Up, Hafiz; grace from high God's face
Beams on thee pure;
Shy then not hell, and trust thou well,
Heaven is secure.

XENOPHANES.

By fate, not option, frugal nature gave
One scent to hyson and to wallflower,
One sound to pine-groves and to water-falls,
One aspect to the desert and the lake,
It was her stern necessity. All things
Are of one pattern made; bird, beast, and plant,
Song, picture, form, space, thought, and character,
Deceive us, seeming to be many things,
And are but one. Beheld far off, they part
As God and Devil; bring them to the mind,
They dull its edge with their monotony.
To know the old element explore a new,
And in the second reappears the first.
The specious panorama of a year
But multiplies the image of a day,
A belt of mirrors round a taper's flame,
And universal nature through her vast
And crowded whole, an infinite paroquet,
Repeats one cricket note.

THE DAY'S RATION.

WHEN I was born,
From all the seas of strength Fate filled a
    chalice,
Saying, This be thy portion, child; this
    chalice,
Less than a lily's, thou shalt daily draw
From my great arteries; nor less, nor more.
All substances the cunning chemist Time
Melts down into that liquor of my life,
Friends, foes, joys, fortunes, beauty, and
    disgust,
And whether I am angry or content,
Indebted or insulted, loved or hurt,
All he distils into sidereal wine,
And brims my little cup; heedless, alas!
Of all he sheds how little it will hold,
How much runs over on the desert sands.
If a new muse draw me with splendid ray,
And I uplift myself into her heaven,

The needs of the first sight absorb my blood,
And all the following hours of the day
Drag a ridiculous age.　　　　·
To-day, when friends approach, and every hour
Brings book or starbright scroll of genius,
The tiny cup will hold not a bead more,
And all the costly liquor runs to waste,
Nor gives the jealous time one diamond drop
So to be husbanded for poorer days.
Why need I volumes, if one word suffice?
Why need I galleries, when a pupil's draught
After the master's sketch, fills and o'erfills
My apprehension?　Why should I roam,
Who cannot circumnavigate the sea
Of thoughts and things at home, but still ad-
　　journ
The nearest matters to another moon?
Why see new men
Who have not understood the old?

BLIGHT.

GIVE me truths,
For I am weary of the surfaces,
And die of inanition. If I knew
Only the herbs and simples of the wood,
Rue, cinquefoil, gill, vervain, and pimpernel,
Blue-vetch, and trillium, hawkweed, sassafras,
Milkweeds, and murky brakes, quaint pipes
    and sundew,
And rare and virtuous roots, which in these
    woods
Draw untold juices from the common earth,
Untold, unknown, and I could surely spell
Their fragrance, and their chemistry apply
By sweet affinities to human flesh,
Driving the foe and stablishing the friend, —
O that were much, and I could be a part
Of the round day, related to the sun,
And planted world, and full executor
Of their imperfect functions.

But these young scholars who invade our hills,
Bold as the engineer who fells the wood,
And travelling often in the cut he makes,
Love not the flower they pluck, and know it not,
And all their botany is Latin names.
The old men studied magic in the flower,
And human fortunes in astronomy,
And an omnipotence in chemistry,
Preferring things to names, for these were men,
Were unitarians of the united world,
And wheresoever their clear eyebeams fell,
They caught the footsteps of the SAME. Our
    eyes
Are armed, but we are strangers to the stars,
And strangers to the mystic beast and bird,
And strangers to the plant and to the mine;
The injured elements say, Not in us;
And night and day, ocean and continent,
Fire, plant, and mineral say, Not in us,
And haughtily return us stare for stare.
For we invade them impiously for gain,
We devastate them unreligiously,
And coldly ask their pottage, not their love,
Therefore they shove us from them, yield to us

Only what to our griping toil is due;
But the sweet affluence of love and song,
The rich results of the divine consents
Of man and earth, of world beloved and lover,
The nectar and ambrosia are withheld;
And in the midst of spoils and slaves, we thieves
And pirates of the universe, shut out
Daily to a more thin and outward rind,
Turn pale and starve. Therefore to our sick
    eyes,
The stunted trees look sick, the summer short,
Clouds shade the sun, which will not tan our hay.
And nothing thrives to reach its natural term,
And life, shorn of its venerable length,
Even at its greatest space, is a defeat,
And dies in anger that it was a dupe,
And, in its highest noon and wantonness,
Is early frugal like a beggar's child:
With most unhandsome calculation taught,
Even in the hot pursuit of the best aims
And prizes of ambition, checks its hand,
Like Alpine cataracts, frozen as they leaped,
Chilled with a miserly comparison
Of the toy's purchase with the length of life.

MUSKETAQUID.

BECAUSE I was content with these poor fields,
Low open meads, slender and sluggish streams,
And found a home in haunts which others
    scorned,
The partial wood-gods overpaid my love,
And granted me the freedom of their state,
And in their secret senate have prevailed
With the dear dangerous lords that rule our
    life,
Made moon and planets parties to their bond,
And pitying through my solitary wont
Shot million rays of thought and tenderness.

For me in showers, in sweeping showers, the
    spring
Visits the valley: — break away the clouds,
I bathe in the morn's soft and silvered air,
And loiter willing by yon loitering stream.
Sparrows far off, and, nearer, yonder bird

Blue-coated, flying before, from tree to tree,
Courageous sing a delicate overture,
To lead the tardy concert of the year.
Onward, and nearer draws the sun of May,
And wide around the marriage of the plants
Is sweetly solemnized; then flows amain
The surge of summer's beauty; dell and crag,
Hollow and lake, hill-side, and pine arcade,
Are touched with genius. Yonder ragged cliff
Has thousand faces in a thousand hours.

Here friendly landlords, men ineloquent,
Inhabit, and subdue the spacious farms.
Traveller! to thee, perchance, a tedious road,
Or soon forgotten picture, — to these men
The landscape is an armory of powers,
Which, one by one, they know to draw and use.
They harness beast, bird, insect, to their
    work;
They prove the virtues of each bed of rock,
And, like a chemist 'mid his loaded jars,
Draw from each stratum its adapted use,
To drug their crops, or weapon their arts
   - withal.

They turn the frost upon their chemic heap;
They set the wind to winnow vetch and grain;
They thank the spring-flood for its fertile
    slime;
And, on cheap summit-levels of the snow,
Slide with the sledge to inaccessible woods,
O'er meadows bottomless. So, year by year,
They fight the elements with elements,
(That one would say, meadow and forest
    walked
Upright in human shape to rule their like.)
And by the order in the field disclose,
The order regnant in the yeoman's brain.

What these strong masters wrote at large in
    miles,
I followed in small copy in my acre:
For there's no rood has not a star above it;
The cordial quality of pear or plum
Ascends as gladly in a single tree,
As in broad orchards resonant with bees;
And every atom poises for itself,
And for the whole. The gentle Mother of all
Showed me the lore of colors and of sounds;

The innumerable tenements of beauty;
The miracle of generative force;
Far-reaching concords of astronomy
Felt in the plants and in the punctual birds;
Mainly, the linked purpose of the whole;
And, chiefest prize, found I true liberty,
The home of homes plain-dealing Nature gave.

The polite found me impolite; the great
Would mortify me, but in vain:
I am a willow of the wilderness,
Loving the wind that bent me. All my hurts
My garden-spade can heal. A woodland walk,
A wild rose, or rock-loving columbine,
Salve my worst wounds, and leave no cicatrice.
For thus the wood-gods murmured in my ear,
Dost love our manners? Canst thou silent lie?
Canst thou, thy pride forgot, like nature pass
Into the winter night's extinguished mood?
Canst thou shine now, then darkle,
And being latent, feel thyself no less?
As when the all-worshipped moon attracts the eye,
The river, hill, stems, foliage, are obscure,
Yet envies none, none are unenviable.

DIRGE.

Knows he who tills this lonely field
To reap its scanty corn,
What mystic fruit his acres yield
At midnight and at morn?

In the long sunny afternoon,
The plain was full of ghosts,
I wandered up, I wandered down,
Beset by pensive hosts.

The winding Concord gleamed below,
Pouring as wide a flood
As when my brothers long ago,
Came with me to the wood.

But they are gone, — the holy ones,
Who trod with me this lonely vale,
The strong, star-bright companions
Are silent, low, and pale.

My good, my noble, in their prime,
Who made this world the feast it was,
Who learned with me the lore of time,
Who loved this dwelling-place.

They took this valley for their toy,
They played with it in every mood,
A cell for prayer, a hall for joy, .
They treated nature as they would.

They colored the horizon round,
Stars flamed and faded as they bade,
All echoes hearkened for their sound,
They made the woodlands glad or mad.

I touch this flower of silken leaf
Which once our childhood knew,
Its soft leaves wound me with a grief
Whose balsam never grew.

Hearken to yon pine warbler
Singing aloft in the tree;
Hearest thou, O traveller !
What he singeth to me?

Not unless God made sharp thine ear
With sorrow such as mine,
Out of that delicate lay couldst thou
The heavy dirge divine.

Go, lonely man, it saith,
They loved thee from their birth,
Their hands were pure, and pure their faith,
There are no such hearts on earth.

Ye drew one mother's milk,
One chamber held ye all;
A very tender history
Did in your childhood fall.

Ye cannot unlock your heart,
The key is gone with them;
The silent organ loudest chants
The master's requiem.

THRENODY.

THE south-wind brings
Life, sunshine, and desire,
And on every mount and meadow
Breathes aromatic fire,
But over the dead he has no power,
The lost, the lost he cannot restore,
And, looking over the hills, I mourn
The darling who shall not return.

I see my empty house,
I see my trees repair their boughs,
And he, — the wondrous child,
Whose silver warble wild
Outvalued every pulsing sound
Within the air's cerulean round,
The hyacinthine boy, for whom
Morn well might break, and April bloom,
The gracious boy, who did adorn
The world whereinto he was born,

And by his countenance repay
The favor of the loving Day,
Has disappeared from the Day's eye;
Far and wide she cannot find him,
My hopes pursue, they cannot bind him.
Returned this day the south-wind searches
And finds young pines and budding birches,
But finds not the budding man;
Nature who lost him, cannot remake him;
Fate let him fall, Fate can't retake him;
Nature, Fate, men, him seek in vain.

And whither now, my truant wise and sweet,
Oh, whither tend thy feet?
I had the right, few days ago,
Thy steps to watch, thy place to know;
How have I forfeited the right?
Hast thou forgot me in a new delight?
I hearken for thy household cheer,
O eloquent child!
Whose voice, an equal messenger,
Conveyed thy meaning mild.
What though the pains and joys
Whereof it spoke were toys

Fitting his age and ken; —
Yet fairest dames and bearded men,
Who heard the sweet request
So gentle, wise, and grave,
Bended with joy to his behest,
And let the world's affairs go by,
Awhile to share his cordial game,
Or mend his wicker wagon frame,
Still plotting how their hungry ear
That winsome voice again might hear,
For his lips could well pronounce
Words that were persuasions.

Gentlest guardians marked serene
His early hope, his liberal mien,
Took counsel from his guiding eyes
To make this wisdom earthly wise.
Ah! vainly do these eyes recall
The school-march, each day's festival,
When every morn my bosom glowed
To watch the convoy on the road; —
The babe in willow wagon closed,
With rolling eyes and face composed,
With children forward and behind,

Like Cupids studiously inclined,
And he, the Chieftain, paced beside,
The centre of the troop allied,
With sunny face of sweet repose,
To guard the babe from fancied foes.
The little Captain innocent
Took the eye with him as he went,
Each village senior paused to scan
And speak the lovely caravan.

From the window I look out
To mark thy beautiful parade
Stately marching in cap and coat
To some tune by fairies played;
A music heard by thee alone
To works as noble led thee on.
Now love and pride, alas, in vain,
Up and down their glances strain.
The painted sled stands where it stood,
The kennel by the corded wood,
The gathered sticks to stanch the wall
Of the snow-tower, when snow should fall,
The ominous hole he dug in the sand,
And childhood's castles built or planned.

His daily haunts I well discern,
The poultry yard, the shed, the barn,
And every inch of garden ground
Paced by the blessed feet around,
From the road-side to the brook,
Whereinto he loved to look.
Step the meek birds where erst they ranged,
The wintry garden lies unchanged,
The brook into the stream runs on,
But the deep-eyed Boy is gone.

On that shaded day,
Dark with more clouds than tempests are,
When thou didst yield thy innocent breath
In bird-like heavings unto death,
Night came, and Nature had not thee, —
I said, we are mates in misery.
The morrow dawned with needless glow,
Each snow-bird chirped, each fowl must crow,
Each tramper started, — but the feet
Of the most beautiful and sweet
Of human youth had left the hill
And garden, — they were bound and still,
There's not a sparrow or a wren,

There's not a blade of autumn grain,
Which the four seasons do not tend,
And tides of life and increase lend,
And every chick of every bird,
And weed and rock-moss is preferred.
O ostriches' forgetfulness!
O loss of larger in the less!
Was there no star that could be sent,
No watcher in the firmament,
No angel from the countless host,
That loiters round the crystal coast,
Could stoop to heal that only child,
Nature's sweet marvel undefiled,
And keep the blossom of the earth,
Which all her harvests were not worth?
Not mine, I never called thee mine,
But nature's heir, — if I repine,
And, seeing rashly torn and moved,
Not what I made, but what I loved.
Grow early old with grief that then
Must to the wastes of nature go, —
'Tis because a general hope
Was quenched, and all must doubt and grope.
For flattering planets seemed to say,

This child should ills of ages stay, —
By wondrous tongue and guided pen
Bring the flown muses back to men. —
Perchance, not he, but nature ailed,
The world, and not the infant failed,
It was not ripe yet, to sustain
A genius of so fine a strain,
Who gazed upon the sun and moon
As if he came unto his own,
And pregnant with his grander thought,
Brought the old order into doubt.
Awhile his beauty their beauty tried,
They could not feed him, and he died,
And wandered backward as in scorn
To wait an Æon to be born.
Ill day which made this beauty waste;
Plight broken, this high face defaced!
Some went and came about the dead,
And some in books of solace read,
Some to their friends the tidings say,
Some went to write, some went to pray,
One tarried here, there hurried one,
But their heart abode with none.
Covetous death bereaved us all

To aggrandize one funeral.
The eager Fate which carried thee
Took the largest part of me.
For this losing is true dying,
This is lordly man's down-lying,
This is slow but sure reclining,
Star by star his world resigning.

O child of Paradise!
Boy who made dear his father's home
In whose deep eyes
Men read the welfare of the times to come;
I am too much bereft;
The world dishonored thou hast left;
O truths and natures costly lie;
O trusted, broken prophecy!
O richest fortune sourly crossed;
Born for the future, to the future lost!

The deep Heart answered, Weepest thou?
Worthier cause for passion wild,
If I had not taken the child.
And deemest thou as those who pore
With aged eyes short way before?

Think'st Beauty vanished from the coast
Of matter, and thy darling lost?
Taught he not thee, — the man of eld,
Whose eyes within his eyes beheld
Heaven's numerous hierarchy span
The mystic gulf from God to man?
To be alone wilt thou begin,
When worlds of lovers hem thee in?
To-morrow, when the masks shall fall
That dizen nature's carnival,
The pure shall see, by their own will,
Which overflowing love shall fill, —
'Tis not within the force of Fate
The fate-conjoined to separate.
But thou, my votary, weepest thou?
I gave thee sight, where is it now?
I taught thy heart beyond the reach
Of ritual, Bible, or of speech;
Wrote in thy mind's transparent table
As far as the incommunicable;
Taught thee each private sign to raise
Lit by the supersolar blaze.
Past utterance and past belief,
And past the blasphemy of grief,

The mysteries of nature's heart, —
And though no muse can these impart,
Throb thine with nature's throbbing breast,
And all is clear from east to west.

I came to thee as to a friend,
Dearest, to thee I did not send
Tutors, but a joyful eye,
Innocence that matched the sky,
Lovely locks a form of wonder,
Laughter rich as woodland thunder;
That thou might'st entertain apart
The richest flowering of all art;
And, as the great all-loving Day
Through smallest chambers takes its way,
That thou might'st break thy daily bread
With Prophet, Saviour, and head;
That thou might'st cherish for thine own
The riches of sweet Mary's Son,
Boy-Rabbi, Israel's Paragon:
And thoughtest thou such guest
Would in thy hall take up his rest?
Would rushing life forget its laws,
Fate's glowing revolution pause?

High omens ask diviner guess,
Not to be conned to tediousness.
And know, my higher gifts unbind
The zone that girds the incarnate mind,
When the scanty shores are full
With Thought's perilous whirling pool,
When frail Nature can no more, —
Then the spirit strikes the hour,
My servant Death with solving rite
Pours finite into infinite.
Wilt thou freeze love's tidal flow,
Whose streams through nature circling go?
Nail the star struggling to its track
On the half-climbed Zodiack?
Light is light which radiates,
Blood is blood which circulates,
Life is life which generates,
And many-seeming life is one, —
Wilt thou transfix and make it none,
Its onward stream too starkly pent
In figure, bone, and lineament?

Wilt thou uncalled interrogate
Talker! the unreplying fate?

Nor see the Genius of the whole
Ascendant in the private soul,
Beckon it when to go and come,
Self-announced its hour of doom.
Fair the soul's recess and shrine,
Magic-built, to last a season,
Masterpiece of love benign!
Fairer than expansive reason
Whose omen 'tis, and sign.
Wilt thou not ope this heart to know
What rainbows teach and sunsets show,
Verdict which accumulates
From lengthened scroll of human fates,
Voice of earth to earth returned,
Prayers of heart that inly burned;
Saying, *what is excellent,*
As God lives, is permanent,
Hearts are dust, hearts' loves remain,
Heart's love will meet thee again.
Revere the Maker; fetch thine eye
Up to His style, and manners of the sky.
Not of adamant and gold
Built He heaven stark and cold,
No, but a nest of bending reeds,

Flowering grass and scented weeds,
Or like a traveller's fleeting tent,
Or bow above the tempest pent,
Built of tears and sacred flames,
And virtue reaching to its aims;
Built of furtherance and pursuing,
Not of spent deeds, but of doing.
Silent rushes the swift Lord
Through ruined systems still restored,
Broad-sowing, bleak and void to bless,
Plants with worlds the wilderness,
Waters with tears of ancient sorrow
Apples of Eden ripe to-morrow;
House and tenant go to ground,
Lost in God, in Godhead found.

HYMN.

By the rude bridge that arched the flood,
Their flag to April's breeze unfurled,
Here once the embattled farmers stood,
And fired the shot heard round the world,

The foe long since in silence slept,
Alike the Conqueror silent sleeps,
And Time the ruined bridge has swept
Down the dark stream which seaward creeps.

On this green bank, by this soft stream,
We set to-day a votive stone,
That memory may their deed redeem,
When like our sires our sons are gone.

Spirit! who made those freemen dare
To die, or leave their children free,
Bid time and nature gently spare
The shaft we raise to them and Thee.